Skateboard Star

Don't miss Catalina's other magical adventures!

Catalina Incognito
The New Friend Fix
Off-Key

BY JENNIFER TORRES

CATALINA INCOGNITO

Skateboard Star

ILLUSTRATED BY
GLADYS JOSE

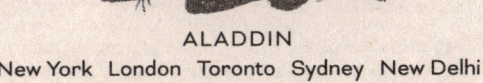

ALADDIN
New York   London   Toronto   Sydney   New Delhi

If you purchased this book without a cover, you should be aware that this book is stolen property. It was reported as "unsold and destroyed" to the publisher, and neither the author nor the publisher has received any payment for this "stripped book."

This book is a work of fiction. Any references to historical events, real people, or real places are used fictitiously. Other names, characters, places, and events are products of the author's imagination, and any resemblance to actual events or places or persons, living or dead, is entirely coincidental.

ALADDIN
An imprint of Simon & Schuster Children's Publishing Division
1230 Avenue of the Americas, New York, New York 10020
First Aladdin paperback edition November 2022
Text copyright © 2022 by Jennifer Torres
Illustrations copyright © 2022 by Gladys Jose
Also available in an Aladdin hardcover edition.
All rights reserved, including the right of reproduction in whole or in part in any form.
ALADDIN and related logo are registered trademarks of Simon & Schuster, Inc.
For information about special discounts for bulk purchases, please contact Simon & Schuster Special Sales at 1-866-506-1949 or business@simonandschuster.com.
The Simon & Schuster Speakers Bureau can bring authors to your live event. For more information or to book an event contact the Simon & Schuster Speakers Bureau at 1-866-248-3049 or visit our website at www.simonspeakers.com.
Designed by Laura Lyn DiSiena
The illustrations for this book were rendered digitally.
The text of this book was set in Century Schoolbook.
Manufactured in the United States of America 1022 OFF
2 4 6 8 10 9 7 5 3 1
Library of Congress Cataloging-in-Publication Data
Names: Torres, Jennifer, 1980- author. | Jose, Gladys, illustrator.
Title: Skateboard star / by Jennifer Torres ; illustrated by Gladys Jose.
Description: First Aladdin paperback edition. | New York : Aladdin, 2022. |
Audience: Ages 6 to 9 | Summary: With the Valle Grande Skate Spectacular competition coming up, Catalina is hoping her sister Coco will win and she can have her old board, but Coco has lost her skateboarding mojo, so Catalina considers entering the competition herself.
Identifiers: LCCN 2022013592 (print) | LCCN 2022013593 (ebook) |
ISBN 9781534483132 (hc) | ISBN 9781534483125 (pbk) | ISBN 9781534483149 (ebook)
Subjects: CYAC: Skateboarding—Fiction. | Sisters—Fiction. | Competition (Psychology)—Fiction. | LCGFT: Sports fiction. | Novels.
Classification: LCC PZ7.1.T65 Sk 2022 (print) | LCC PZ7.1.T65 (ebook) |
DDC [Fic]—dc23
LC record available at https://lccn.loc.gov/2022013592
LC ebook record available at https://lccn.loc.gov/2022013593

For Ava Mae, magical already

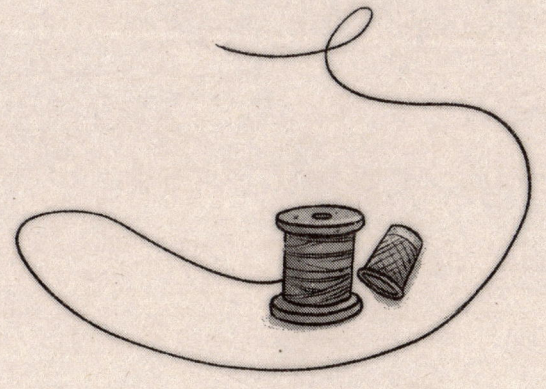

Contents

CHAPTER 1	Skateboard Slump	1
CHAPTER 2	Lucky Shirt	9
CHAPTER 3	Unprepared	17
CHAPTER 4	Incognito	25
CHAPTER 5	A Surprise Package	34
CHAPTER 6	Sewing Magic	41
CHAPTER 7	Skateboard Star	47
CHAPTER 8	Sew Disappointing	55
CHAPTER 9	Worn and Torn	62
CHAPTER 10	Small Steps	70
CHAPTER 11	A Perfect Fit	74
CHAPTER 12	A New Journey	83

· CHAPTER 1 ·

Skateboard Slump

I sharpen my colored pencils into perfect points and arrange them in rainbow order, just like I do every Saturday morning. That way, they are always ready when I need them.

I'm working at the kitchen table so that my baby brother, Carlos, who is rolling toy trucks on the floor with Papi, doesn't disturb me. You can't be too careful with Carlos around. I've found his tiny teeth marks on my school supplies before!

Right as I am about to place parakeet green next to lemon yellow, my big sister stomps past and bumps into my shoulder. She knocks my hand into the box of colored pencils and sends them tumbling to the floor.

"Coco!" I yell. She has never appreciated the importance of a good organization system. But that doesn't mean she can ruin mine. "Watch out!"

"Sorry, Cat," Coco says. She is carrying her skateboard and sets it down to help me pick up the pencils. At first, I try to keep them all in rainbow order. But then Carlos comes crawling toward us, drool dribbling off his bottom lip. I scramble to collect the rest of them as quickly as I can.

"What's the rush, Coco?" Papi asks as he scoops

Carlos back onto his lap. Mami won't be back from her shift at the nursing home until dinnertime.

Coco puts the candy-apple-red pencil next to the midnight-blue one, nowhere near where it belongs. "Can I go out skateboarding?" she asks.

She is already wearing her helmet and pads, and her old flannel shirt is balled up under her arm. It's going to be a wrinkled mess when she puts it on.

"Have you made your bed?" Papi asks.

"Of course!" Coco replies.

"Ha!" I bark.

Coco's idea of making the bed is piling her pajamas, sheets, and blanket on top of it in a lumpy heap. I should know. I have to share a room with her.

But Papi seems convinced. "Have fun," he says. "Be careful."

I take the red pencil out of the box and put it back where it's supposed to be—next to tangerine orange. "Wait up," I say. "Give me a minute to put the rest of these pencils away, and I'll come too."

Coco has been helping me learn to skateboard. Since all my chores are finished—including some that Mami and Papi didn't even think of—I can go with her to learn some new tricks.

"No!" Coco says.

"No?" I repeat. Coco doesn't always let me borrow her board, but she's never said I couldn't come with her to skate.

"I really need to concentrate this time," she says. "I need to be alone."

I turn to Papi. "Por favor. Pleeeeeeeease," I say, begging in two languages.

It doesn't work.

"Sorry, Kitty-Cat," Papi says. "Sounds like Coco needs her space."

Being called "Kitty-Cat" is pretty annoying. I've

asked my parents about a zillion times to start using my real name, Catalina. But even more annoying is not getting to go out with Coco. I grab the pencil box and storm upstairs to our room.

Not that I plan to stay there.

As soon as I hear Coco's skateboard rattle down the sidewalk, I go to my closet. I pick out my favorite sweatshirt. It's gray with kitten ears sewn onto the hood. My tía abuela—her name is Catalina Castañeda too—sewed it for me. Normally I wouldn't wear it. Like I keep telling my Mami and Papi, I'm getting too old for all the kitten stuff. But today the sweatshirt is exactly what I need.

I creep back down the stairs, tiptoe through the hall, and sneak out the side door.

Then, flattening myself against the house so that no one can see, I put on the sweatshirt. I zip it up to my chin. I pull the hood over my head. A shiver runs up my spine. I check my reflection in one of the windows. A gray cat blinks back at me. I am incognito.

Tía Abuela didn't make the sweatshirt with a regular needle and thread. She used a special sewing kit with the power to create magical disguises. Better yet, she passed the magic on to me!

I trot down the street to find Coco. She might have said I couldn't watch her skateboard, but she didn't say anything about a *cat* watching.

I find Coco at the end of the block. She must really not want anyone to see her.

I can understand why. She's wearing her flannel, but it's way too short, and her elbow pokes out of a hole in the sleeve. I shudder. I wouldn't want to be seen in that thing either.

Then again, Coco doesn't care very much about what anyone else thinks of her clothes. Something else must be bothering her. I step closer and stop to watch under the shade of a blue mailbox.

Coco tightens her helmet. She wipes her palms against her shorts and takes off.

I recognize this move. It's her signature trick, the Coco-kick. She steps down onto the back of the board and launches it into the air. Next she's supposed to flick the board with her toe so it spins underneath her. Instead she kicks it off to the side and lands on her knees.

Ouch.

She tries an easier trick, one she has landed millions of times. But she just keeps crashing.

"What's going on?" I ask. Only, I'm still incognito and it comes out like a curious purr. Coco lifts her head off the sidewalk where she's still sprawled.

"I was hoping nobody saw that," she said. "But you won't tell, will you?" She sits up and scoots closer to me. "You seem familiar. Have I seen you before?"

I skitter backward.

Coco shakes her head and unbuckles her helmet. "I need to land the Coco-kick for the Skate Spectacular," she says. "It has to be perfect. But I can't seem to get anything right. I might as well go home."

Home? Uh-oh.

CHAPTER 2

Lucky Shirt

I race back home. If Coco were riding her skateboard, I'd have no chance of beating her there. Luckily for me, she's carrying the board as she trudges back, her face turned down to the sidewalk. I glance over my shoulder, and she's still two houses behind when I throw open the side door and race through the kitchen.

"Gato!" Carlos says, waving.

Oh no! I'm still wearing the magical disfraz, and

Carlos thinks I'm a cat! It's a good thing Papi is too busy warming noodles on the stove to notice.

"And what does a gato say?" he asks.

"Miau!" Carlos shouts.

I bound up the stairs, yanking off the sweatshirt. When I get to the bedroom, I grab a book off Coco's side of the floor, open it to a page in the middle, and dive onto my bed. I pretend to be deep in concentration when Coco walks in.

"Oh . . . hi!" I greet her, still a little out of breath. "How was . . . skateboarding?"

Coco grimaces. "What happened to you?"

"What do you mean?" I ask.

She points. "Your face. Your hair. Your *shoes*."

I touch my cheek—warm and sweaty. I pat my hair—curls tangled. I glance down at my feet—shoes still on, even though I'm on the bed. Usually I am perfectly put together.

"I guess I got carried away with the story," I fib. "I just got to a really good part."

Coco tilts her head and squints at the book cover. I turn it over and look too.

Amazing Math Puzzles.

It's one of the books Papi uses in the class he teaches at the community college. Whoops.

Coco tosses her flannel at me. "Well, if you're not too busy, do you think you can fix this?"

The shirt lands on my lap. Fixing it would mean I'd have to . . . touch it.

Coco's favorite flannel used to be a bright green-and-purple plaid. Now it's faded into a brownish-grayish color. Besides the hole in the elbow, it's missing two buttons, and the pocket is torn off on one side.

"Why don't you wear one of the new ones Mami bought you?" I ask. Mami has been trying for months to get Coco to replace her flannel. But the new ones just hang in her closet, unworn.

Coco flops down onto my bed, wrinkling the blanket. Now I'll have to make it all over again.

"You *know* why!" she says. She takes one of my stuffed animals and hugs it against her chest. "That is my lucky shirt. It's the one I was wearing when I landed my first trick."

I know the flannel is special to her, but it's time to retire it.

"What makes you think I can fix this?" I lift the tattered cloth with my pinkie.

"Tía Abuela gave you that sewing kit, didn't she?" Coco answers.

Coco doesn't know that the sewing kit is magical. I nod.

"And you've been going to all those sewing classes at the library, haven't you?"

Coco means Stitch and Share. Tía Abuela used to be a famous actress. Ever since she retired, she spends most of her time traveling the world. Since she wasn't going to be in town to teach me to sew, she made me promise to attend the weekly Stitch and Share sessions her best friend, Josefina the Librarian, hosts at the Valle Grande Central Library.

I haven't missed a single session. "The magic is only as strong as your stitches," Tía Abuela warned when she gave me the sewing kit for my birthday. If I was going to be in charge of such powerful magic, she wanted to be sure I had plenty of practice.

But I don't think Coco's grungy old flannel is what she had in mind. It's not what I have in mind either.

"Maybe your luck will jump onto one of the other shirts," I tell her.

Coco shakes her head. "There's not time to find out," she explains. "The Valle Grande Skate Spectacular is coming up, and the first-place winner gets a new skateboard. I can't afford to take any chances."

"But you already have a skateboard," I say, trying to mask how much I wish *I* had a skateboard of my own.

Coco rolls over so she's staring at me. Her eyes glimmer. "Don't you get it?" she says. "If I get a new one, I can give my old one away."

I sit up straighter, almost bumping my head on the top bunk. "To me?" I ask. If I had my own skateboard, I'd never have to borrow from Coco again. I could ride it whenever I wanted to. In my mind, I'm already peeling off all those stickers she's plastered onto the bottom.

"Maybe," Coco replies. "But I can't give it to you if I don't win, and I can't win unless my lucky shirt gets fixed."

I pick up the flannel again. Maybe it's not so hideous after all.

· CHAPTER 3 ·

Unprepared

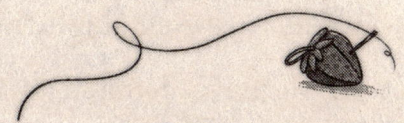

*A*fter school on Monday, I take Coco's flannel to the Stitch and Share session at the Valle Grande Central Library. During Stitch and Share, Josefina the Librarian opens the library community room so all the sewists—that's what Josefina calls us—can get together and work on our latest projects and practice our skills.

There are always plenty of people around to help if I run into any trouble. I'm sure the sewists will have great ideas for fixing Coco's flannel.

"Early as usual, Catalina," Josefina says when I push open the door and walk in. She is carrying a big plastic bin full of sewing supplies and scraps of fabric that people have donated to the library. We can take anything we need from the bin. When I first started coming to Stitch and Share, the bin was so full that Josefina couldn't get the lid to stay on. Now it's almost empty.

"Right on time to help set up," I reply. Punctuality is one of my specialties. Early for Josefina the Librarian is perfect timing for me. I start arranging the folding chairs in a circle. That way, all the sewists can talk and see what everyone else is working on.

Being the first to arrive also means I get to pick the one chair that doesn't have any dents or scratches or spilled paint from library art projects on it. I like my sewing station to be as perfectly put together as I am.

I settle in and open my sewing bag. I made it myself out of a pattern that was originally meant to be a pillowcase. It's made of a leopard-print fabric that Josefina picked out of the scrap bin for me.

"I thought it would be *purr-fect* for a fierce *cat* like you," she said. "Get it?"

Normally I would have reminded Josefina that I don't really like all that cat stuff as much as I used to when I was younger. But leopard print happens to be one of Tía Abuela's favorite patterns, so I made an exception.

I lift Coco's flannel out of the bag. I'd convinced her to let me wash it, promising that the luck wouldn't rinse out. The shirt is still faded. At least it smells a little better.

But as soon as the rest of the sewists arrive and

everyone else takes out their projects, mine seems dingier and dirtier than ever.

Piled on Señora Garcia's lap is a heap of shimmering blue satin and gold lace.

Mr. Hart has a piece of checkered wool that I can already tell is going to turn into a hat.

Even Anthony Becerra, the only other kid in the group, has brought something special. Anthony is in high school, and he's been working on dog and cat toys to donate to the animal shelter as part of a service project. But today he takes out a whole dog bed!

I fold Coco's flannel into the tiniest possible bundle. I wish I had a disfraz so that no one would see me.

I have never felt so unprepared. It's an even worse feeling than falling off Coco's skateboard.

Josefina the Librarian claps. "Bueno!" she says. Good. "I see you're all ready for the Spring Sewing Showcase, and you didn't even need me to remind you. Looks like we are going to have some beautiful projects to share this year."

I raise my hand but don't wait for Josefina to call on me. "Sewing showcase?" I ask.

Josefina walks toward me. "How could I forget?" she replies. "This will be your first showcase, won't it, Catalina?"

I nod. It sounds very important.

"Well, every spring, we sewists put together a display of our work," Josefina explains. "We also collect donations from people who come see it, and use the money to buy new sewing supplies. This year

I'm hoping we can raise enough to buy a sewing machine for the library!"

Señora Garcia smooths the blue satin over her lap. "I'm making a gown for my niece's quinceañera," she says, smiling.

"Keen-seh-ahn-YEHR-uh?" Mr. Hart repeats the word slowly.

"It's a fifteenth-birthday party," I tell him.

Then Mrs. Glass shows us the tiny squares of fabric she's sewing together. "And I am trying out a new quilt pattern."

Josefina sits in the seat next to mine. "What have you brought to work on?"

I unfold Coco's flannel, wishing I had something better.

"I told my sister I would help her repair this," I say. "But don't worry. I'll think of something *way* better for the showcase." I want to help raise money for sewing supplies too.

Josefina takes the shirt and examines it. "You know," she says, "there are beautiful mending techniques that you could show off. Some people even make their repairs visible on purpose."

They *want* people to see what's wrong with their clothes? It seems impossible, but Josefina shows me pictures on her phone as proof.

Ms. Yoo pats her knee. "I sewed a patch onto these jeans, and I like them even better this way."

It's not that I don't believe them. But a showcase project has to be something special. Something surprising. Something *perfect*.

Coco's flannel is simply not going to cut it.

· CHAPTER 4 ·

Incognito

How am I going to fix Coco's flannel in time for the Skate Spectacular *and* sew up an amazing project for the showcase?

I hate to admit it, but I'm going to need help from Pablo Blanco.

Pablo is my best friend—and biggest rival—at Valle Grande Elementary School. No one else in third grade is as perfectly prepared as we are.

I plan my outfits a week in advance. Pablo brings

a spare change of clothes to school every day, socks and everything, just in case something spills at lunch.

I keep a color-coded calendar. Pablo schedules his weekends down to the minute.

He'll help me find a way to solve this problem. But when I explain Coco's skating slump, he says, "Don't you see? This is exactly like what happened in *The Kitchen Curse*!"

The other important thing to know about Pablo is that he is a major fan of telenovelas, the kind of super-dramatic TV shows that Tía Abuela used to star in before she retired.

I scrunch my nose. "Pablo, I don't think anyone put a *curse* on my sister—"

"Just listen," he says, interrupting me. He's so excited that he is standing on the tips of his toes. His white sneakers are spotless as usual. "What if one of the other skateboarders has *sabotaged* Coco, done something to spoil her chances so she can't win. That's what happened to Chef Marcela on last night's episode. Her jealous assistant, Salvador, cut the power to her oven right in the middle of the prince's banquet! Dinner was ruined!"

"Hmm," I say. I am not convinced that anyone is playing tricks on Coco. But just to be sure, Pablo

and I have agreed to meet at the skate park where she sometimes practices after school.

"To spy?" I ask Pablo.

"To *observe*," he says.

We crouch underneath a picnic table on a grassy hill above the park. We're a little far from the edge of the emptied-out pool where Coco and her friends are getting ready to skate. It's a good thing Pablo has brought his binoculars.

One by one, the skateboarders drop into the bowl. They gain speed as they sail down the smooth walls. Usually Coco flies out in front, swooping back and forth from one end of the pool to the other.

But this time, she hangs back. She twists the piece of hair that falls out from under her helmet. She doesn't even look like herself without her lucky flannel. It's

still hanging in my closet, waiting to be fixed.

Finally Coco rolls to the edge of the pool. She leans over and looks toward the bottom. Slowly she lets the board tip over, and she glides down.

"It's about time," I mutter. I wasn't sure she was *ever* going to drop in.

But then, before she's even reached the bottom, Coco jumps off and stumbles to a stop. The skateboard rolls away without her.

"Muy interesante," Pablo says, setting down his binoculars.

"*What's* interesting?" I ask. "Did you see anyone push her? Did someone mess with her skateboard?"

Pablo shakes his head. "No," he says. "It's that Coco is even worse off than I thought. Maybe you'd be able to see that for yourself if *you'd* come prepared." He glances at the binoculars.

"I'm going to get a closer look," I say with a huff as I

stand and shake the grass off my legs. "You stay here."

The truth is, I *did* come prepared. Prepared with something even better than binoculars. But I can't let Pablo see it.

I knew a disfraz might come in handy today. But I couldn't use my kitten hoodie. If Coco caught me in it again, she might get suspicious. Instead I set my alarm for extra early this morning so I could whip up a new disguise. It's in my backpack, folded inside a paper bag labeled *súpersecreto*, super secret.

I skip down the hill, darting from tree to tree so that Coco and her friends don't see me. When I get to the skate park entrance, I duck behind a vending machine. I unzip my backpack and remove my disfraz: a yellow pillowcase that I turned into a dress. I also sewed three black stripes across the middle so that when I slip it over my shoulders and step out from behind the vending machine, I am incognito. A bumblebee!

The other skateboarders scatter as I whiz by them.

"Look out, it's a bee!" one of them shouts.

Another swats at me. "Go away!"

I dodge and almost slip into the pool.

Coco doesn't flinch, though. She's never been afraid of bees. Then again, she's never been afraid of the staircase feature at the skate park either. Yet here she is, standing in front of it looking like she is too scared to go on.

I remember what she always tells me. "Just *try*," I say. It comes out like a buzz.

Then, almost as if she's heard me, Coco tightens her helmet. "You've got this," she tells herself.

"You do!" I buzz. Coco steps onto the board with one foot and pushes off with the other. She rolls toward the bottom step. I expect her to pop the skateboard up and to slide along its edge.

"Go, Coco!" But my cheer quickly turns into a cringe. Coco doesn't jump high enough, and instead of landing on top of the step, she crashes into it. The skateboard skids away in one direction while she stumbles in another.

"I don't know what's wrong with me," Coco says, rubbing her elbow. "I just can't do it anymore."

I gasp. Pablo was right! Someone *is* sabotaging Coco. But it's not one of the other skaters. It's *her*! Coco hasn't lost her luck. She's lost her *confidence*.

· CHAPTER 5 ·

A Surprise Package

Pablo waves his arms in frustration as we leave the park. "How can you be so sure the other skateboarders aren't behind this?" he asks. "I didn't see you anywhere near them, and I was looking." He pats his binoculars, which hang from a strap around his neck.

I can't tell Pablo the truth—that I actually *was* right next to Coco and the others. That would mean giving away the secret of the magic sewing kit. I shrug instead.

"Just a hunch," I say.

• SKATEBOARD STAR •

We split up at the corner. Pablo walks to his house, and I go to mine, the bumblebee disfraz tucked safely into my backpack.

I think about all the skateboard tricks Coco used to do. She was never afraid of trying out new jumps and twists. Maybe I can inspire her by attempting a big trick of my own—not with a skateboard but with a sewing needle.

As soon as I get home, I race to my desk and take out my notebook and colored pencils. (Luckily, they're still sharpened. It pays to be prepared.) Then I sketch out a new design. When I'm finished, I take it downstairs and ask Mami for help dialing Tía Abuela on video chat.

No matter where she's traveling, Tía Abuela always tries to pick up when I call.

I take the tablet to the couch in the living room and wait for her face to appear on the screen.

Bleeeeep.

Bleeeeep.

I'm not sure just where in the world Tía Abuela might be. Her travels are sometimes a mystery. Maybe it's too late for her to talk.

But then, right as I'm about to press the red button that ends the chat, she answers.

"Kitty-Cat? Is that you?" she says. "Qué sorpresa!" What a surprise.

A breeze is blowing Tía Abuela's silver hair off her face. Even though it looks like the sun is beginning to set, she wears cat-eye sunglasses with sparkling rhinestones in the corners. Just like always.

I catch a flash of red feathers in the trees behind her.

"Where are you?" I ask, leaning in closer to the screen.

"Belize, of course," she answers. "It's the best

time of year for bird-watching. I can't wait to show you my pictures. Qué pasa?" What's happening?

I tell Tía Abuela about the Sewing Showcase. How I want to impress the other sewists—and raise money for Stitch and Share.

Tía Abuela's cherry-red lips part in a dazzling smile. "I'm sure my comadre Josefina can help you come up with the perfect project." "Comadre" is what Tía Abuela calls Josefina the Librarian because they have been such good friends for such a long time.

But I don't need Josefina to help me think up a project.

"I already have an idea in mind," I say with a wink. "An *exciting* idea. But I need your help."

One of Tía Abuela's eyebrows lifts over the top of her sunglasses.

I hold my notebook up to the camera and unveil my sketch. "The Dragon Dress . . . two-point-oh."

The Dragon Dress is one of Tía Abuela's most famous costumes. It's a long, emerald gown, with gleaming red and orange gems at the neck. Tía Abuela sewed it herself, and it's on display in the Valle Grande library lobby. I can already picture my own, smaller version standing next to it.

"I think I have enough fabric left over from the box you sent me," I explain. "And I can use glitter from the library craft stash for the gems. But I'm not sure where to start."

I expect Tía Abuela to shout with excitement. I expect her to say, *Sí! Of course I'll help!* After all, she's the one who taught me my first stitch.

Instead she presses her lips together. "Remember,

Catalina, I sewed that dress after many years of practice. Don't be discouraged if you're not able to make it yet."

My shoulders fall. "Don't you think I can do it?"

Tía Abuela takes off her sunglasses. Her long eyelashes flutter as she blinks at me. "I know you can do it . . . someday," she says. "I also know that you don't need a dress to impress anyone. Your progress is what's most impressive. It reminds me of an old saying."

Tía Abuela has lots of old sayings.

"A camino largo, paso corto," she recites.

I can understand a little Spanish, but sometimes I need help. "What does that mean?"

"For a long journey, take small steps," Tía Abuela translates. "Learning to sew is a long journey. Be proud of the steps you have taken so far."

I try to hide my frown, but I can't. If you're on

a long journey, shouldn't you take *big* steps? To get where you're going faster?

"I'll send you a package," Tía Abuela says. "Something that will help."

That's exactly what I was hoping for. Maybe she'll send a dress pattern, or maybe some jewels to add to my design. I know better than to ask, though. Tía Abuela loves surprises.

Just then Coco bursts through the front door. I look up. She's carrying her skateboard. "You said you'd fix my flannel, Cat!" she says. "Are you finished yet? I really need it."

Mami glances up from the crossword she's working on while she waits for a pot of water to boil on the stove. "A promise is a promise, Kitty-Cat," she says.

I turn back to Tía Abuela. "Better go," I say.

Tía Abuela winks and says, "Adiós!"

· CHAPTER 6 ·

Sewing Magic

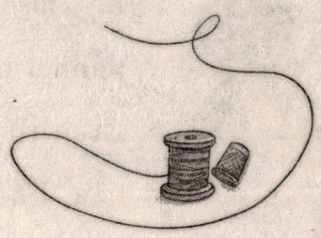

I'd rather start sewing my gown. But, like Mami said, I *did* promise. At least mending the flannel will give me extra practice while I wait for Tía Abuela's package to arrive.

There's also another good reason to work on the shirt: I still want Coco's old skateboard, and I won't get it unless she wins the Skate Spectacular.

I'm not sure fixing the flannel will help. But I don't know how else to get Coco's confidence back.

I march upstairs and open the door to my closet. I pull Coco's flannel off the hanger. Even though it's clean now, I keep it separate from the rest of my clothes. Like I said, you can't be too careful.

Next I gather my supplies and take them to my desk. I have collected a lot since I started sewing over the summer: thimbles and measuring tape from Tía Abuela, ribbons and thread from the sewists at Stitch and Share, and even a new pair of scissors that I bought with saved-up allowance money.

I keep all of it inside the practice sewing kit Tía Abuela left me. This one isn't magical. But it's *sort of* incognito. It's made out of an old tin of butter cookies!

Now that I'm properly prepared, I inspect the shirt, trying to figure out where to start. Replacing the missing buttons will be easiest, I decide.

I open the cookie tin and push supplies around until my fingers land on two spare buttons. A red one I snipped off a shirt that doesn't fit anymore and a shiny gold one I found on the walk to school.

The buttons don't match, but I don't think Coco will mind. Just look at her cluttered closet or the stacks of crumpled paper on her desk. She might even like the shirt better this way.

When I first started sewing, it took me forever just to thread the needle. Now I finish sewing on the new buttons before Mami has even called me down for dinner.

The shirt is already looking much better. Like

it's not about to fall apart in my hands. I decide to move on to the pocket.

I snip some thread off a brown spool that's in the cookie tin. That will blend in with the fabric best. Maybe no one will even notice the tear.

Then I change my mind. I decide to follow Josefina's advice. Instead of trying to hide the repair, I will make it stand out.

"Orange," I say to myself as I choose a different spool.

For this repair, I use a stitch I've just learned: the backstitch. Josefina said it's very strong, which is exactly what Coco needs to keep this shirt in one piece.

When I'm done, there is a neat line of orange dashes along one side of the pocket. Perfect.

The shirt is looking so good now that a new idea pops into my mind. One I never expected. What if I *try on* Coco's flannel? I'm curious to know what's so special about it, and maybe wearing the shirt will help me fix it. I glance at the door to make sure it's shut. Coco will never even know.

Quickly I carry the shirt to my closet, where a mirror hangs on the back side of the door. I push my arms through the sleeves, first the right, then the left.

I tug it over my shoulders.

I straighten the collar.

I check my reflection.

It's a perfect fit!

I twist and turn in front of the mirror. Even though the flannel *is* old—and even though my elbow is poking through that hole in the sleeve—I don't want to take it off. I puff out my chest. I stick up my chin. Coco was right all along. Something about this shirt makes me feel stronger. Braver. *Luckier*.

That's when I realize something. Maybe I don't need Coco to win the Skate Spectacular in order for me to get my own skateboard. Maybe I can win it myself—with a little bit of sewing magic.

• CHAPTER 7 •

Skateboard Star

I have to wait until it's Saturday again to test out my latest creation.

Coco lounges on the sofa, an arm and a leg hanging off the edge. Since I've already finished organizing my colored pencils, I am trying to show Carlos different ways to sort his blocks: by color, by shape, and by size. It's never too early to learn good organizational skills.

Carlos doesn't seem to agree, though. He throws

one of the blocks, and it lands on the pile of math tests Papi is grading. Papi sighs and rolls it back to Carlos.

"You're not going to go out skateboarding, Coco?" Papi asks.

Coco yawns. "What's the point?" she replies. "I'll never get out of this slump."

Papi scratches his forehead. "That doesn't sound like the Coco I know."

He's right. Coco hasn't even nagged me about her flannel lately. Which is a good thing, since I'm kind of hoping to keep it for myself.

"Well, you can't sit on the couch all day," Papi continues. "Why don't you take your brother for a walk in his wagon? He could use some fresh air. I have a feeling you *both* could."

Coco groans and rolls off the sofa. She puts on her shoes, then picks up Carlos and heads for the side door.

"You're not going with them, Kitty-Cat?" Papi asks.

"I want to, but I . . . umm . . . ," I sputter, trying to think up an excuse. "I have to finish something upstairs."

It's the truth. But only part of the truth. The flannel still needs one last touch, and with Coco out of the house, I finally have a chance to finish it.

I hurry upstairs before Papi can ask any more questions. Better get stitching.

This time, I don't use the cookie tin sewing kit. I reach for the other one. The *magic* one.

I keep it on the top shelf of my closet, and it doesn't look like anything special. It's an old pouch

made of red velvet, almost as worn-out as Coco's flannel. Inside is a brass thimble, a needle stuck into a strawberry-shaped pincushion, and a spool of silver thread—all the tools I need to sew a magical disguise.

Then I grab Coco's shirt and a patch I made out of a piece of black felt. It's shaped like a cat. It even has whiskers! Normally I wouldn't choose cat accessories *on purpose*, but I don't want anyone to mistake me for Coco when I'm wearing the disfraz. I want them to know it's me. Me, but better. A skateboard star.

I place the patch over the rip in the elbow and stitch it on with the silver thread. When I've gone all the way around, I tie a knot at the end to seal the magic.

The disfraz is ready. I put it on, and my spine tingles.

I am incognito. Kind of.

Coco and Carlos will be back soon, so I have to hurry. I race downstairs, out the door, and to the garage, where I find my helmet and Coco's skateboard.

I take a deep breath and roll out to the sidewalk.

Two of Coco's friends are across the street. When I see them, I put my foot down to stop the skateboard. They've laughed when I've fallen before. I'm not sure I can skate in front of them again. But it's the only way to know if the disfraz is working.

I step back onto the board and push off.

"You've gotten a lot better, Cat," Coco's friend Trish says when I get to the other side of the street.

"Yeah," her other friend, Albert, agrees.

Have I actually gotten better? Or do they only think so because of the disfraz? I gulp. Coco's friends almost never talk to me. I don't know what to say.

"So where's Coco?" Trish asks.

"She's out for a walk with our brother," I reply.

Trish steps back to make room for me on the sidewalk. "We're practicing our pop shove-its," she says. "Want to try?"

Trish jumps onto her board and rolls toward the curb. When she gets to the edge, she steps down on the tail of the skateboard, popping up the nose as she hops over. The board rotates front to back before she lands on top of it again.

"Your turn," Albert says.

I back up. I might look like an expert skater, but I'm really not.

"Come on, Cat," Trish says. "Let's see what you can do."

There might be *one* trick I can show them, something Coco has been teaching me. It's not as exciting as Trish's, but it's a small step. Like what Tía Abuela said.

I turn my skateboard wheels-up on the sidewalk and slide my feet underneath it. Then, as I jump, I flick the skateboard over with my toes and stomp on top of it, right side up.

"Nice!" Trish says.

Albert holds up his hand for a high five.

If the magic flannel works on the judges the same way it seems to be working on Trish and Albert, I just might win after all!

The rattling of wagon wheels interrupts my daydream. Uh-oh. I turn around.

"You were supposed to be fixing that shirt for *me*," Coco shouts. "Why is there a *cat* on it?"

• CHAPTER 8 •

Sew Disappointing

"Buenas tardes!" Papi calls out when Coco and I get home from school. She brushes by me without a word.

I step through the door and kick off my shoes. "Buenas tardes," I reply. But nothing feels very good about this afternoon.

Even though it's been more than a week, Coco still isn't speaking to me. It isn't *just* that I sewed that cat-shaped patch onto her flannel (although, she's pretty annoyed about that, too). It's that when she tried to put the shirt on again, it wouldn't fit over her shoulders. It must have shrunk in the wash!

"A package arrived for you," Papi says.

"It did?" I had almost given up hope. All of a sudden, the afternoon is looking *much* better. I run upstairs, hang up my backpack on its special peg in my room, and race back down to find Papi.

"Where is it?" I ask, panting. "The package?"

Before he can answer, I begin rummaging through the pile of mail he has stacked on the kitchen counter. I don't even bother to keep things in order the way I normally do.

Papi chuckles. "You must be expecting something pretty important."

Pretty important? That's an understatement.

"Only the *most* important thing I can think of," I tell Papi.

That's because the Dragon Dress 2.0 is not coming out the way I hoped it would. The silky green fabric I'm using is so slippery that I can't cut it in a straight line. Nothing is quite the right size even though I measured *three* times. Measuring is usually one of my specialties.

But just like me, Tía Abuela always has impeccable timing. If that package is from her, it couldn't have arrived at a more perfect moment. The Sewing Showcase opens this weekend. I'm sure she has sent me exactly what I need to save my dress.

"I set the package aside for you on the coffee table," Papi said. "I had a feeling you would be excited to open it."

I spin around on my heel and head straight for the living room. There's a brown envelope, right where Papi said it would be. And, just like I'd hoped, the stamp on the front says it came from

Belize. Even Tía Abuela's handwriting looks magical, with loopy letters written in shiny gold ink.

But the envelope is smaller than I was expecting. Part of me wished Tía Abuela would send me a finished dress. She probably thought that would be cheating, though. I shake the envelope. Maybe there are new sewing tools inside. Or a new spool of magical thread.

Carlos comes crawling in from the kitchen. "Mine?" he says, reaching for the envelope. I pull it away. *Whatever's* inside, I can't have his sticky hands all over it.

Finally I tear open the envelope, turn it upside down, and shake it out. A note flutters onto the coffee table, but I don't bother reading it yet. I'm too busy finding what else is in the envelope.

It's a surprise, all right. A big one. But not the good kind.

What I pull from the envelope is nothing like what I thought it might be. It's a scrap of fabric, with a line of messy, uneven stitches on it. They are so loose and crooked that it takes me several seconds to realize the stitches are *mine*. This is the piece of fabric Tía Abuela gave me to practice on when she taught me the running stitch for the first time.

They are the *opposite* of perfectly put together.

There must be some mistake, I think. Tía Abuela's surprise was supposed to *help* me with my showcase project. All this does is make me think about how terrible I used to be when I first started sewing.

I don't remember Tía Abuela's note until I notice

Carlos pulling himself up on the edge of the coffee table and grabbing it. I snatch it back from him a moment before he puts it into his mouth.

I unfold the thin piece of pink paper. It smells like oranges—one of Tía Abuela's favorite scents. No wonder Carlos thought it was a snack.

Querida Catalina, the note begins. *This is probably not the gift you were expecting.*

Not even close.

But before you get disappointed [too late for that!], *remember that the sewing kit was not what you expected either. In the end, it was more special than you realized.*

I keep reading.

Even if your dress doesn't turn out the way you imagined, you should be proud of how far you've come. I know I am! I hope these stitches remind you of where you started and inspire you to go even further.

I look down at the stitches again. The only thing they inspire me to do is hide them. I stuff the piece of fabric into my pocket.

At least it's Monday. That means there's a Stitch and Share session. If Tía Abuela won't help me with my showcase dress, I know the other sewists will.

· CHAPTER 9 ·

Worn and Torn

*E*ven though I still feel bad that it doesn't fit Coco anymore, I plan to wear the flannel to Stitch and Share. I tell myself it's because I want to show Josefina and the other sewists my mending work. That's partly true, but it's not the only reason. I also want the burst of confidence I feel when I wear the shirt.

I need all the confidence I can get if I'm going to finish my gown. Especially now that Tía Abuela's surprise turned out to be such a flop. I'm starting to get nervous that I'm not as prepared to sew the Dragon Dress 2.0 as I thought I was.

I fold the silky green fabric pieces and pack them into my sewing bag, along with all my supplies. Since I know it's going to take a lot of work to finish the dress, I arrive at the library even earlier than usual. The community room is still empty, and the lights are off. I switch them on and spread the pieces of my dress out in the middle of the floor to examine them.

It's even worse than I thought.

I managed to sew the sleeves, but one is longer than the other. The bottom of the skirt is all crooked. The edges are beginning to fray.

"Catalina?"

"Aah!" I jump up, startled. But when I turn around to see who's there, it's only Josefina the

Librarian. She's carrying the fabric bin, and it's even emptier than it was last time.

"You're here early," Josefina continues. "Even for you." She looks down at my green fabric pieces. "What's all this?"

Now that my breath has slowed down, I kneel on the floor again. I explain my plan to recreate Tía Abuela's Dragon Dress in a size that would fit me.

"I bet lots of people would come to see it, and that would help you raise money for the sewing machine," I say. "I wanted to surprise you and the other sewists with the finished dress, but I'm having a little trouble." I frown. Even with all my practice, I can't seem to sew this dress.

Josefina sets the bin down on the desk at the back of the room. She comes back and sits on the floor next to me.

"You designed the dress yourself?" she asks.

I open my sewing bag and take out the notebook. I flip the pages until I get to the sketch I made of the dress, the one I showed Tía Abuela earlier.

Josefina takes the notebook and peers down at my drawing. Her glasses slide down her nose. Does she see something wrong with it?

"Hmm," Josefina says. "It takes a lot of creativity to design a dress like this. You have great attention to detail. Look at the sparkles on that collar!"

I take the notebook back. I already knew I have great attention to detail. That's why Tía Abuela trusted me with the sewing kit. But somehow the dress still turned into a major mess.

Josefina picks up one of the sleeves. "And you made the pattern on your own?"

I nod. "I didn't have a pattern, so I traced around one of the dresses I already had."

Josefina claps. "Good thinking!" she says. "Sometimes sewists have to be problem solvers. You have excellent problem-solving instincts."

But if I'm such an excellent problem solver, why is my dress in pieces?

Josefina puts the fabric down. She squeezes my shoulder. "This was a very *ambitious* project," she says. "That means you took on a big challenge, something much more difficult than anything you've ever sewn before. You should be proud."

I look down at the pile of green fabric on the floor and wrinkle my nose. "Proud of *that*?"

"Por supuesto," Josefina says. Of course. "And you should keep at it. If you try again next year, I bet you'll get even further."

Next year? "But I need to finish by Saturday!" I protest. "Otherwise I won't have a project to display in the Sewing Showcase!"

If Josefina can't help me, then none of the other sewists will be able to either.

I drop my head to my chest and fiddle with one of the new buttons I sewed on to Coco's flannel. It doesn't budge. My stitches are good and strong. Still, the shirt doesn't give me the burst of confidence that it did before.

"That's not Coco's old shirt, is it?" Josefina asks. "I almost didn't recognize it." She points to the patch on my elbow. "I love how you repaired that hole." I am not surprised. Josefina is a cat lover. Even her watch has a cat on it. The hour and minute hands are whiskers.

I look up, and when I do, Josefina notices the orange stitches on the pocket.

"Just look at that backstitch!" she exclaims. "I can see you've been practicing."

I can't hold back a smile, even though I'm still pretty disappointed.

"You know," Josefina goes on, "one of the most special things about knowing how to sew is being able to fix what's worn and torn. Why not use this shirt as your showcase project? People would learn a lot from it."

I shrug. "I'll think about it," I mumble. My eyes begin to sting. I pack up my fabric and all my supplies. For the first time since I started sewing, I *don't* stay for Stitch and Share.

· CHAPTER 10 ·

Small Steps

*E*verything is falling apart, even worse than Coco's flannel was before I fixed it. I haven't helped my sister find her confidence again—I've only made her more upset.

As if that's not bad enough, I still don't have a project for the showcase. And now there isn't enough time, or enough fabric, to try again. Not even the magic sewing kit will help.

I stop in front of a trash bin on my way home and

lift the lid. I want to throw away the Dragon Dress—more like Dragon *Disaster*—so I never have to look at it again. But when I take one of the sleeves out of my sewing bag, I notice my stitches. I didn't realize before how straight and even they are.

I drop the trash can lid and dig into my pocket for the fabric scrap Tía Abuela sent. I compare my first stitches to my latest. They are so different that I almost can't believe I sewed both of them. This must be what Tía Abuela meant by taking small steps. I couldn't see how those small steps had added up—how far I've come—until I remembered where I'd started.

For the first time, I begin to feel a little better about the Dragon Dress 2.0. *And* about my sewing. Josefina is right. By next year, I'll make even more progress. I can't wait to see what my stitches look like then.

I jog the rest of the way home, in a hurry to talk

to Coco. Maybe if I remind her how far she's come too, she won't be so frustrated about all the trouble she's been having lately. Maybe she'll get some of that old Coco confidence back.

Only, she isn't outside practicing when I get home. Her skateboard is leaning against the side of the garage where I left it the other day. I sit down next to it and wriggle out of the flannel.

I could try to give it back to Coco. If I snip off the cat-shaped patch, it might feel like hers again. But she still won't be able to wear it. It doesn't fit anymore. Anyway, what will happen when it gets so worn-out that even I can't fix it?

Coco needs something that will last, that she can't ever outgrow. That she can carry around with her like the line of stitches I'm carrying in my pocket.

That's when I get another idea. My best one yet. Even better than the Dragon Dress 2.0.

I pull the cookie-tin sewing kit out of my bag and fish around inside for the scissors. It would be easier (not to mention tidier) to do this upstairs at my desk. But Coco might be there, and I want to surprise her.

I hold the shirt in one hand and the scissors in the other. I hesitate. If I go through with this, I won't be able to use the flannel as my Sewing Showcase project, even if I want to.

I also won't be able to wear it as a disfraz to impress the judges at the Skate Spectacular.

But Coco will.

I make the first cut.

· CHAPTER 11 ·

A Perfect Fit

It's the morning of the Skate Spectacular. I am pacing outside my bedroom with my sewing bag slung across my chest. My palms start to sweat, and *I'm* not even the one who is going to be late.

In fact, I woke up a whole hour earlier than usual to make sure I'd have enough time to get ready. When the alarm went off, I let it *brrrring* for two whole minutes, hoping it would wake Coco up too.

It didn't. She rolled right over and kept on

snoring. Coco could sleep through anything.

Including the Skate Spectacular if she doesn't wake up soon! I check my watch. Coco has exactly twenty-nine minutes to roll out of bed, get dressed, eat breakfast, and make it to the skate park in time for the competition.

Mami and Papi told me not to bother Coco. They said she needs her rest. But she'll never make it on time unless I do something. I wish I could put on the bumblebee disfraz. If I were incognito, I could buzz into the room and sting Coco out of bed without Mami and Papi even knowing.

I look down at my watch again. Twenty-*eight* minutes. That's it. I look right down the hall, then left toward the stairs, to make sure Mami and Papi aren't watching. When I'm sure they're not, I tiptoe into my room and grab a pillow off my bed.

With the pillow tucked under one arm, I climb

the ladder to the top bunk. I lift the pillow over my head to clobber Coco with it. But before I can bring it down, Coco raises herself up on an elbow and pulls out one of her earbuds.

"What are you doing?" she asks.

I let the pillow fall, sort of disappointed that I didn't get to use it. "You're awake," I say.

"Of course I'm awake. It's almost ten o'clock," Coco replies, as if she is *always* up at this time.

She is not.

"Then why are you still in bed?" I ask. If I had to sleep in Coco's bed, I'd jump out of it as soon as I could every morning. It's full of stray socks and who knows what else. "You should be getting ready for the Skate Spectacular. It's going to start without you."

Coco flops back down onto her pillow.

"Doesn't matter," she says. "I'm not going."

I had a feeling she might say that. After all, she hasn't been practicing all week.

As usual, I am prepared.

I sit at the edge of Coco's bed. I try not to think about how long it's been since she washed the sheets.

"But you've worked so hard," I tell her. "Don't you want to show everyone what you can do?"

Coco groans. "I still can't land the Coco-kick," she says. "And now that my lucky flannel doesn't fit anymore, I might never do it again."

This is the perfect moment. I reach into my sewing bag and take out Coco's flannel. What's left of it anyway.

"What if you could have your flannel back?" I ask, waving the cloth in front of her.

Coco sits straight up. She frowns. "What did you do to it?"

Uh-oh. Maybe I should have asked first.

The other day, leaning against the garage, I cut a big square out of the back of the shirt. That's the section that was the least faded and the least worn-out. I folded the square in half diagonally and turned it into a triangle. Then I sewed the two loose edges together with my strongest and neatest stitches.

"I turned it into a bandana!" I announce. "Now you'll never outgrow it. You'll always be able to keep it with you as a reminder of where you started. So what if you don't land the Coco-kick today? You've still come so far, one step at a time."

Coco snatches the bandana from my hands and stares at it. Our room is so quiet, I can hear the ticking of my watch. With each second that passes, I have to bite the inside of my cheek a little harder to stop myself from telling Coco to HURRY.

"I fell a lot before I landed that first trick," she

says finally. "But I stuck with it. Maybe that's what I need to do now."

She ties the bandana around her neck. It's a *perfect* fit. Thanks to my attention to detail.

"Does this mean you're going to skate in the competition?" I ask.

"If you ever get out of the way," she answers. "You're blocking the ladder."

I scramble down and check my watch. I gasp. "You only have twenty-one minutes to get there!"

Coco jumps down from the second-to-last wrung. Her confidence is already starting to come back, I can tell.

"*I* only have twenty-one minutes?" she says. "Aren't you coming too?"

Even though it's almost time for the Sewing Showcase, I can't miss Coco's comeback. Mami and

Papi and I pack Carlos into his wagon and race after her toward the park.

She's the last skater to arrive.

"You made it," says the woman at the check-in station.

"Right on time," Coco says with a grin.

"Hardly," I mutter. But I'm smiling too.

We find a spot to sit on the grass while Coco joins the other skaters. When her name is announced, I watch Coco push off and glide down a ramp. It's not the fastest I've ever seen her, but at least she doesn't jump off this time.

Coco zigzags around the park, then hops up onto a rail. So far, so good.

Mami whistles. Papi and Carlos clap.

I'm too nervous to join them—it's nearly time for the Coco-kick.

Coco builds up speed. She steps down hard on

the back of the board and rockets upward. But she doesn't get high enough for the board to spin all the way around before she comes down again. She lands crooked, with one foot on the ground.

Oh no. I twirl a curl tight around my finger, worried that Coco will be disappointed.

But after she yanks her helmet off, she pumps her fist in the air and shouts, "I'm back!"

Finally I can cheer. Even if she doesn't win the competition, Coco has beaten her skateboard slump. That's a big step.

I start to race down the hill to congratulate her.

"Shouldn't you get to the library?" Papi asks. "You're going to be late."

Impossible. I'm never late. I look down at my watch. The Sewing Showcase opens in five minutes!

"See you later, Kitty-Cat!" Mami yells. I'm already racing to the library.

• CHAPTER 12 •

A New Journey

Pablo Blanco is already standing at the library entrance when I arrive. I frown. I was hoping I could still get here before him.

He's tapping his foot as if he has been waiting outside for *hours* instead of only a few minutes.

"It's about time you got here," he says. "The showcase opened four minutes and forty-seven seconds ago."

On the outside, I roll my eyes. But inside I'm

happy that Pablo is here. Even if he *is* being a little persnickety. I'm still nervous about my showcase display, and it feels better having a friend here with me.

"Well, let's not stand here wasting even more time," I say. "Let's go inside."

Pablo sniffs in reply. He puts his nose in the air and walks into the building. I march in behind him.

Everything is all set up in the community room. I realize I'm even more excited to see the other sewists' projects than I am to show off my own. But first we stop at the donation jar that Josefina has set on a table near the entrance. Each of us drops some coins inside.

I try to count up the money in the jar and wonder if it's enough to buy a sewing machine. But before I'm finished, Pablo grabs my wrist.

"Are those puppies?" He yanks me over to Anthony Becerra's project. "You never said there were puppies at Stitch and Share."

Usually there aren't. Josefina the Librarian gave Anthony special permission to bring some dogs from the animal shelter to the showcase opening. They're playing inside a small pen. One gnaws on a purple chew toy.

"I made that!" I tell Pablo. It's one of the toys we helped Anthony make for the animal shelter.

Nearby, two puppies nap on one of Anthony's pet beds. "They look very comfortable," I say.

"Gracias!" Anthony replies. He can't talk long.

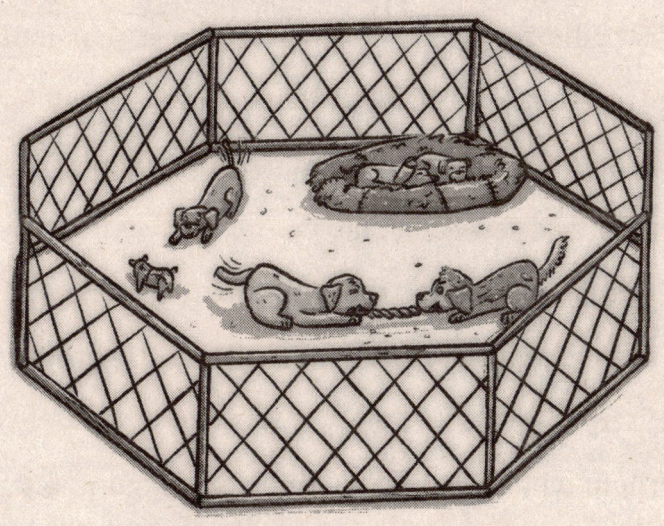

Someone is waiting to order a handmade pet bed from him!

Pablo leans in close and whispers, "Did he really make that himself?"

I nod.

I expect him to say it reminds him of something he once saw in a telenovela, but he doesn't. Instead he whistles. "Maybe I should learn to sew too."

And maybe *I've* just recruited Stitch and Share's newest member.

We admire the tiny pieces of fabric that make up Mrs. Glass's quilt. Both Pablo and I can tell how much attention to detail it must have taken to carefully cut and sew each one.

Next we check out the collection of puppets Ms. Yoo sewed, and Mr. Hart's finished cap. He even lets Pablo try it on.

Then, when we see Señora Garcia's quinceañera

gown, with its shimmering satin and piles of fluffy tulle, Pablo gasps. "This is even better than the costumes on the new show Mom and I are watching!"

Josefina the Librarian chuckles as she walks up to us. "Catalina! Pablo!" she says. "I see you're enjoying the showcase."

I point to the donation jar. It's filling fast. "Looks like you'll have enough to buy lots of new supplies for Stitch and Share," I say.

Josefina grins. "That means lots more practice for you," she agrees. "Have you shown Pablo *your* project yet?"

I was saving it for last.

I lead Pablo to the table where my display is set up.

"Did you finish the Dragon Dress two-point-oh?" he asks, walking a little faster. Tía Abuela happens to be Pablo's favorite actor. He was probably looking forward to seeing my replica of her gown.

"Not exactly," I admit. "I need more time to get it right. So I came up with something different. What do you think?"

I emptied my craft bin—and used every single one of my colored pencils—to make a poster board that shows my sewing progress so far.

Pinned on one side is the fabric scrap Tía Abuela sent, the one with my very first stitches. On the rest of the board, I've displayed examples of the projects I've worked on in Stitch and Share: one of the dozens of pillowcases Josefina made me sew, a drawstring pouch, the vest I made to wear in the talent show, and even the butterfly wings that were part of a magical disfraz. (I hope no one notices the silvery thread that sparkles a little more brightly than it should.)

At the top of the poster board I've written "My Sewing Journey."

Pablo's eyes widen. He presses his lips together.

I can tell he's trying hard not to smile. He squints. "Pretty good," he says. "But I bet I could sew even neater stitches."

I laugh. "You could try, but you'd better start practicing."

Just then I hear the familiar whir of rolling wheels. I snap my head around. It's Coco! She's still wearing her lucky bandana.

I'm about to tell her that she shouldn't be riding her skateboard inside the library. It's against the rules. But then I look down and notice she's not riding her skateboard. She's riding a new one.

"You won?"

Coco leaps off the board and pops it up into her arms. "I won! I didn't land the Coco-kick perfectly, but no one else even attempted it."

Pablo frowns and scoots away, but I throw my arms around Coco's neck and hug her.

"Let's go celebrate at the skate park," she says. "Your new board is parked right outside. I even brought your helmet."

My new board? I can't wait. I turn to Pablo. "Want to come?"

He shakes his head. "I think I'm going to stay and take another look at that hat," he says. "I might want to make one myself."

I'm sure he can do it. Someday.

"Don't forget," I call over my shoulder as I follow Coco out the door. "It's going to be a long journey. Just take it one small step at a time."

Turn the page for a sneak peek at Catalina's first magical adventure!

Attention to Detail

The picture on the puzzle box shows three gray kittens peeking out of a picnic basket.

Kittens. Of *course*.

If Mami and Papi didn't give me a kitten puzzle for my birthday, they would give me a kitten sticker collection. And if they didn't give me a kitten sticker collection, they would give me a kitten coloring book. Even though they know I am getting too old for all this kitten stuff. And even though I have told them to quit calling me "Kitty-Cat" and start using my real name, Catalina.

Everyone in my family—Mami and Papi; Baby Carlos in his high chair; my big sister, Coco; and Tía Abuela—is sitting around the kitchen table. They all lean forward, watching me.

"Well, Kitty-Cat," Papi asks, "what do you think?"

The first thing I think is, *Quit calling me "Kitty-Cat."*

But that's not what I say, because the *second* thing I think is that even though I don't love kittens as much as I used to, I still love puzzles. You get to figure out exactly where each piece belongs, and when you're finished, you know you haven't made any mistakes.

"It's perfect," I say.

"Maybe we can work on it together," Mami suggests.

Carlos claps. A droplet of drool drips off his lip and onto the high chair tray. I picture it landing on my puzzle. I fold my arms over the box to protect it from even the *idea* of Carlos's baby slobber.

"Hmm," I reply. Not quite a yes, and not exactly a no.

Luckily, Coco slides her gift across the table before I have to give a real answer.

She has wrapped it in this morning's newspaper. And lots and lots of tape. I don't have to open it to know what's inside—her old skateboard helmet.

"I'll even let you borrow my board," Coco says. She pulls the brim of her baseball cap lower down on her forehead. It hides her eyes, but not her smirk. "Unless you're still too scared after what happened the first time."

"I am *not* scared," I say, but my cheeks go warm

as I remember last summer's wipeout.

Papi slaps his hands on the table. "Bravo, Coco!" he says. "Did you hear that, Kitty-Cat? Your sister is going to teach you to skateboard."

I don't need Coco to teach me, I think. This year I am ready. This year I will be perfect.

"Thank you, *Consuelo*," I say. I make my voice as sweet as a sip of horchata on a sunny afternoon. "You are *too* generous."

At last it is time to open Tía Abuela's gift. Tía Abuela's gifts are always the best.

Tía Abuela is Papi's aunt—my great-aunt—and her name is Catalina Castañeda too.

Only, most people know her as "La Chispa," the spark, one of the rottenest villains in telenovela history. Before she retired, the characters she played on TV were awfully, monstrously, fabulously *bad*. The rich but cruel stepmother. The beautiful but wicked duchess. The evil twin. Fans say her acting was so amazing, it was as if she *transformed* into every character.

Tía Abuela doesn't visit our house on the hill in Valle Grande very often. She's too busy traveling the world. But she always sends souvenirs home to my brother and sister and me.

Tía Abuela is only in town for the grand opening of the Catalina Castañeda Children's Room at the Valle Grande Central Library. The library was her favorite place to visit when she was growing up. It's where she first learned all about heroes and villains and adventures.

She's also here to celebrate my birthday, of course.

She has just returned from exploring the ancient Mayan city of Palenque in Mexico. Her gift comes in a box, wrapped in shimmering gold paper and a purple ribbon. I try to imagine what's inside. "An archaeologist's hand shovel?" I guess. "Ooh! I know, a map of the jungle!"

But when I untie the ribbon, tear apart the paper, and open the box, I don't find either of those things.

What I find instead is a red velvet pouch. It isn't new. Not even *almost* new. In fact, the pouch is so ancient, the cloth is worn bald in places.

It reminds me a little of an old dog with patchy fur. I try not to wrinkle my nose.

I know I should smile.

I know I should say "Thank you."

I know I should say *something*.

But I worry that if I so much as twitch, the groan I am trying to swallow will come tumbling out of my mouth before I can stop it.

"Not what you were expecting?" Tía Abuela says with a snort.

Not even close.

But it would be rude to just say so. So I don't.

I open the pouch and peer inside. There is a little brass thimble, a spool of silver thread, and a needle poking out of a strawberry-shaped pincushion.

Nope. Definitely not what I was expecting.

"Cata*lina* . . ." Mami nudges me with her voice. It's my name, but it is also a warning.

I try to think of something polite to say. "Thank you, Tía Abuela. It is so . . . so . . . so *different*."

Tía Abuela cackles. "Do you even know what it is, Kitty-Cat?"

I shake my head.

"It is a sewing kit. I've had it since I was your age. I thought it was the perfect gift for someone with your . . . How shall I put this?" She pauses. She taps a flamingo-pink fingernail against her lips as she thinks of the right thing to say. "Someone with your *attention to detail*. Attention to detail is very important when it comes to sewing."

"Hmm" is all I say.

Looking for another great book?
Find it
IN THE MIDDLE.

Fun, fantastic books for kids
in the in-be**TWEEN** age.

IntheMiddleBooks.com

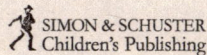 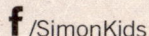 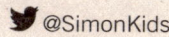

READ & LEARN

with *simon kids*

Keep your child reading, learning, and having fun with Simon Kids!

A one-stop shop where you can **find downloadable resources, watch interactive author videos, browse books by reading level, and more!**

**Visit us at
SimonandSchusterPublishing.com/ReadandLearn/**

And follow us @SimonKids

 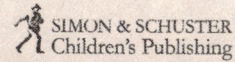 

Off-Key

Don't miss Catalina's other magical adventures!

Catalina Incognito
The New Friend Fix
Skateboard Star

BY JENNIFER TORRES

CATALINA INCOGNITO

Off-Key

ILLUSTRATED BY
GLADYS JOSE

ALADDIN
New York London Toronto Sydney New Delhi

If you purchased this book without a cover, you should be aware that this book is stolen property. It was reported as "unsold and destroyed" to the publisher, and neither the author nor the publisher has received any payment for this "stripped book."

This book is a work of fiction. Any references to historical events, real people, or real places are used fictitiously. Other names, characters, places, and events are products of the author's imagination, and any resemblance to actual events or places or persons, living or dead, is entirely coincidental.

ALADDIN
An imprint of Simon & Schuster Children's Publishing Division
1230 Avenue of the Americas, New York, New York 10020
First Aladdin paperback edition July 2022
Text copyright © 2022 by Jennifer Torres
Illustrations copyright © 2022 by Gladys Jose
Also available in an Aladdin hardcover edition.
All rights reserved, including the right of reproduction in whole or in part in any form.
ALADDIN and related logo are registered trademarks of Simon & Schuster, Inc.
For information about special discounts for bulk purchases, please contact
Simon & Schuster Special Sales at 1-866-506-1949 or business@simonandschuster.com.
The Simon & Schuster Speakers Bureau can bring authors to your live event. For more information or to book an event contact the Simon & Schuster Speakers Bureau at 1-866-248-3049 or visit our website at www.simonspeakers.com.
Designed by Laura Lyn DiSiena
The illustrations for this book were rendered digitally.
The text of this book was set in Century Schoolbook.
Manufactured in the United States of America 0622 OFF
2 4 6 8 10 9 7 5 3 1
Library of Congress Control Number 2021945046
ISBN 9781534483101 (hc)
ISBN 9781534483095 (pbk)
ISBN 9781534483118 (ebook)

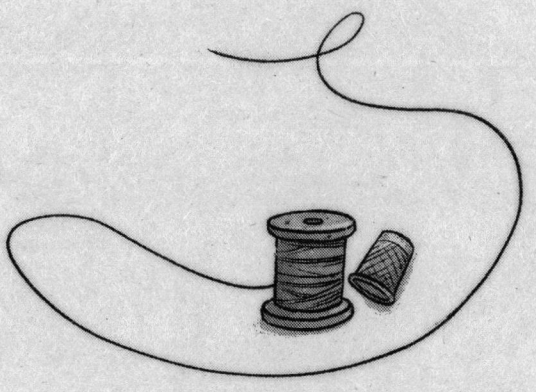

Contents

CHAPTER 1	*Flutter*	1
CHAPTER 2	*Special Delivery*	10
CHAPTER 3	*Following Instructions*	20
CHAPTER 4	*Just Right*	32
CHAPTER 5	*Extra Help*	41
CHAPTER 6	*In the Spotlight*	48
CHAPTER 7	*Solo*	56
CHAPTER 8	*Incognito*	64
CHAPTER 9	*Sew Busy*	72
CHAPTER 10	*Even Better*	79
CHAPTER 11	*A Perfect Performance*	86

· CHAPTER 1 ·

Flutter

It's after school on Monday, and the auditorium is filled with students practicing for the Valle Grande Elementary talent show. Auditions are at the end of this week.

I creep past a group of fourth graders tap-dancing side by side next to a second grader performing a tae kwon do demonstration.

Behind them, Aaron Chu, a third grader in my class, rehearses his magic act. He swooshes his cape.

He waves his hands over a black top hat. He taps the edge of the hat with his wand. I watch, waiting to see what will happen.

When nothing does, Aaron peers into the hat and shrugs.

I shudder. I'd hate for *my* act to go wrong. That's why I'm sneaking through the auditorium. Somewhere in this room is the formula for a perfect performance, and I'm going to find it. I need to make sure my group has an amazing audition and gets picked for the show.

The best part is, none of the other kids notice me. Not really. When they look in my direction, all they see is a yellow-winged butterfly. That's because last summer my tía abuela—her name is Catalina Castañeda too—gave me a special sewing kit.

It might not *look* very special, just an old, worn-out velvet pouch. But the needle and thread inside have the power to sew magical disguises.

Over the weekend, I sewed butterfly wings onto one of my old sweaters. (It was missing a button anyway. I could have sewn on a new one, but it wouldn't have matched the others, and I can't stand it when things don't match.) Then I added antennae to one of my hairbands. The perfect disfraz! Now anyone who sees me thinks I'm a butterfly. I am *incognito*.

Tía Abuela told me to save the magic for times when I *really* need it. Once my spool of silvery magical thread is gone, it's gone for good.

This is one of those times when I need my magic. After all, my bandmates and I will be performing a song that Tía Abuela made famous back when she was still a telenovela actress. We can't make any mistakes.

I flutter behind Esme Galindo and her cousin

• Jennifer Torres •

Jazmín. They wear swirling blue skirts as they practice a folklórico dance.

Suddenly Jazmín stops in the middle of a step.

"What happened?" Esme asks. "Did you forget what comes next?"

They definitely need more practice.

Jazmín shakes her head. "No, but I thought I saw Catalina."

Uh-oh. Maybe my disfraz isn't working. I duck behind a cardboard tree some fifth graders are using as a prop in their skit.

"Shouldn't she be with her own group?" Esme asks.

"You know Catalina," Jazmín continues. "She probably wanted to give us some of her helpful hints."

Esme giggles, and they start dancing again.

I *might* have a reputation for being a bit of a perfectionist. *Who doesn't want to be perfect?* I almost wonder aloud. Instead I look over my shoulder to make sure the butterfly wings are still attached.

Tía Abuela warned me that the magic would only be as strong as my stitches. And these are coming loose! I need to get out of this disfraz before anyone else notices!

While the fifth graders argue over their lines,

I yank off the wings and slip out of the sweater. I tuck everything under my arm, then step out from behind the carboard tree and find my group at the other side of the auditorium.

We call ourselves Banda La Chispa in honor of Tía Abuela. Her fans know her as La Chispa, "the spark," because she was always so bright and dazzling onscreen.

Ruthie Rosario sits behind her drum set. Soledad Beltrán has her guitar strapped over her shoulder. Pablo Blanco, my best friend—and biggest rival—stands next to his keyboard, tapping his foot. He scowls when he sees me. "You're late," he says.

Impossible. No one cares about punctuality as much as I do. Except for Pablo, that is. I look down at my watch and frown. Unfortunately, he's right.

"Only thirty-six seconds," I say.

"Thirty-seven," Pablo argues. "And anyway, late is late. Where were you?"

I hesitate. So far I haven't revealed the secret of the magic sewing kit to anyone.

Luckily, Ruthie interrupts before I have to answer.

"Cool hairband!" she says. "Animal accessories are my favorite!"

I feel the top of my head. I'm still wearing the butterfly antennae. "Um, thanks," I mumble, my cheeks going all warm. Pablo snorts. Normally I am perfectly put together.

Soledad hands me the tambourine we borrowed from the music room. "Now that we're all here," she says, "let's run through the song from the very beginning."

Ruthie taps out the rhythm with her drumsticks.

"Uno, dos, tres, cuatro!" Soledad counts. She begins to strum, then nods at Pablo, who presses down on the keys. I start shaking the tambourine. When we get to the chorus, I open my mouth to sing. Only, I can hardly keep up with Ruthie's beat.

Pablo's notes clash with Soledad's chords, and we all sound a little . . . off-key.

When the song ends, I cringe. Part of me wants to run back to that cardboard tree to hide again. Maybe we can still back out of the auditions. Then I remind myself of something Tía Abuela taught me when I was first learning to sew: progress takes practice. *And* patience. Sometimes a *lot* of patience.

"Don't worry," I reassure everyone. "We still have a few more days to get better."

"Are you kidding?" Soledad shouts. "That was amazing! And so much fun! We are obviously going to make the talent show."

But I'm not so sure.

CHAPTER 2

Special Delivery

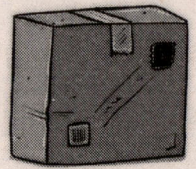

I can't open the door at first when I get home from school. Something is blocking it. My older sister, Coco, probably dumped her enormous backpack in the entryway. *Again.* This is exactly why I asked Mami to install those special hooks on our bedroom wall. I thought that if the backpacks had a special place to hang, maybe Coco would stop leaving hers on the floor. It doesn't seem to be working.

"Co—" I start to complain as I shove the door

open. Then I look down. It isn't Coco's backpack that's blocking the way. It's a big box. Addressed to me! The postage on top says it came from Colombia.

And the handwriting tells me who sent it: Tía Abuela.

Ever since she retired from acting, Tía Abuela spends most of her time traveling the world. Wherever she goes, she finds a way to send packages home to Valle Grande. Last time, it was stickers for Coco's skateboard. And the time before that, a hand-carved rattle for Baby Carlos, our little brother. This time, it's something for me.

I push the box into the living room, where Papi and Coco are putting on a puppet show for Carlos. Maybe they should audition for the talent show too.

"It's about time you got home," Coco says.

"We almost couldn't resist opening that box," Papi agrees.

Carlos claps his hands, all sticky with the applesauce he's been snacking on. I wrinkle my nose and make a mental note not to let him touch whatever's inside the package.

"Well, what are you waiting for?" Coco asks, leaping up from the carpet and flinging the dinosaur puppets off her hands. "Open it!"

Of course I'm going to open it. But first I need the proper tools. Calmly I carry my backpack to the coffee table and set it down. I unzip the middle pouch and take out my school scissors.

Coco groans.

Then I carefully snip the tape along one side of the box. I am about to move on to the next piece of tape when Coco nudges me aside.

"This is going to take forever!" she complains. She kneels beside the box and rips off the rest of the tape with one sharp tug. "There. It's open."

I want to tell Coco that patience makes perfect, but I am just as excited as she is to see what Tía Abuela sent. I lift open the cardboard flaps. The gift is wrapped in tissue paper, with a note card sitting on top.

I take the note card out of the box and read aloud. *"Mi amiga Josefina tells me you are making excellent progress with your sewing. Keep practicing! Sewing can be like magic. But remember what I've told you. The magic is only as strong as your stitches."*

I can imagine Tía Abuela winking behind her cat-eye sunglasses when she wrote those lines. I glance up to see if Papi or Coco suspect that Tía Abuela was writing about *real* magic. They don't, so I keep reading. *"I wanted you to have some new material for your next projects. This fabric is from the fashion shows in Medellín. I can't wait to see what you create with it!"*

· OFF-KEY ·

I set the note card down and reach into the box. Underneath the tissue paper are bundles of fabric. One piece is icy blue and speckled with silver stars. The largest piece is purple and satiny smooth. There's a zebra print—one of Tía Abuela's favorite patterns—and a piece that shimmers with pink and gold sequins.

Papi takes a velvety green square and uses it to play peekaboo with Carlos. I'm so dazzled by all the fabric that I don't even mind him touching it. *Much*.

"She didn't say anything else?" Papi asks after his next *Boo!* "Nothing about where she's traveling next?"

"I don't think so," I answer. She hardly ever does. Sometimes we try to guess where her next postcard will come from, but it's always a surprise. Papi should know that.

Then Coco picks up the note card. "She did! There's more writing on the back!"

I yank the note from her hand. Coco is right. I can't believe I missed it. Most of the time, I have excellent attention to detail. It's why Tía Abuela trusted me with the magic sewing kit in the first place. I read on. *"Maybe you can show me what you're working on when I come to visit. Your papi told me you'll be singing in the school talent show. I wouldn't miss it! You know the old saying: 'Quien canta sus males espanta.' 'Whoever sings frightens their worries away.'"*

"Is this true?" I ask when I get to the end.

Papi tilts his head and thinks for a moment. "Well, singing *does* put me in a good mood," he says. "So I suppose it's true."

"I'm not asking if the *saying* is true!" I reply. "I mean what Tía Abuela wrote before that. Is it true she's coming to visit?"

Papi laughs. "Surprise!" he says. "I knew Tía Abuela would love to hear you sing. Especially since you'll be performing one of her songs."

Coco takes the zebra-print fabric and whips it around her neck like a cape. "I can finally show her my kick flip!" she exclaims. "And Tía Abuela promised to bring back pictures of the big skate parks in South America."

Even Carlos starts to clap again.

Not me. I sit there, staring at the note.

"What's the matter, Kitty-Cat?" Papi asks. "Aren't you excited to see Tía Abuela?"

I can tell him at least one thing that's the matter: he won't stop calling me "Kitty-Cat." As I've told my family about a zillion times, I'm getting too old for all this kitten stuff.

But that's not *really* what's bothering me. *Of course* I'm excited to see Tía Abuela. I'm especially excited to show her how far my sewing has come. When she started to teach me over the summer, I could barely thread a needle.

But this news has made me even *more* nervous about the talent show audition. What if Banda La Chispa doesn't get picked for the show, and Tía

Abuela travels all this way for nothing?

Or worse, what if we *do* get to perform, and we're terrible?

"I'm excited," I tell Papi finally. "But the band has a lot of practicing to do. *And* I need to get to Stitch and Share."

· CHAPTER 3 ·

Following Instructions

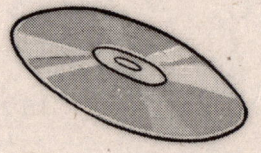

When she gave me the magic sewing kit, Tía Abuela made me promise to go to the Stitch and Share sessions that her best friend, Josefina the Librarian, holds once a week at the Valle Grande Central Library. If I'm going to be responsible for such powerful magic, Tía Abuela wants to make sure I learn how to use it.

As usual, I am the first to arrive. Most of the time, Josefina arranges metal folding chairs in a circle in the library's community room. One by one, we sewists—that's what Josefina calls us—choose a seat and take out our latest project. We share what we're working on, and there's always someone to give advice if we get stuck.

But today I notice something different: a table at the center of the room with a piece of fabric spread over it. Josefina smooths out the wrinkles, then arranges pieces of thin crinkly paper on top. They look a little like puzzle pieces. I am excellent at putting puzzles together. Figuring out exactly where things belong is one of my specialties. Maybe this time *I* can help Josefina for a change.

"What are you working on?" I ask.

"Catalina!" she greets me. "Early as usual. I'm tracing a pattern for a dress I want to sew. Come watch."

I step closer to the table and study the pieces.

"It doesn't *look* very much like a dress," I say before I can stop myself. I slap a hand over my mouth, hoping I haven't made Josefina feel bad.

She laughs and picks up one of the pieces. "Not yet," she agrees. "But soon this will be a sleeve."

She takes the paper and gently drapes it around my arm.

"See?" she asks.

I look down at the pattern piece on my arm and then at the rest of the pieces. I close my eyes and picture them stitched together instead of flat on the table. The dress comes together in my imagination.

"I see it!" I say.

Josefina smiles and places the sleeve pattern back on the fabric. She shows me how to carefully trace around its edge with a chalk pencil to create a sleeve-shaped piece of cloth. She even lets me cut out the piece that will become the dress's skirt. I love following directions step-by-step and making my cutting line smooth and straight.

This might be my favorite Stitch and Share session yet!

But then, as the other sewists begin to arrive and choose their seats, Josefina does something that makes me gasp. The skirt should have been the last pattern piece, but Josefina isn't finished. She uses the chalk pencil to draw a teardrop shape on the fabric and cuts that out too.

"That's not supposed to be there!" I protest. You don't get to add your own pieces to a puzzle. They would have no place to fit. A dress shouldn't be any different from a puzzle. "Isn't that breaking the rules?"

Josefina chuckles again. "Don't worry, Catalina," she says. "I add pockets to all my dresses. That way I can always carry kitty treats with me." She pats the side pocket of the pants she's wearing. "You never know when the library might have another feline visitor."

I gulp. One of the cats that Josefina found wandering in the library was really *me* wearing a magical disfraz.

Luckily, Josefina doesn't seem to suspect anything. She goes on. "Do you know what my favorite part of sewing is?"

"Obviously it's not paying attention to the instructions," I mumble.

"No," Josefina replies. "It's getting the chance to give whatever I create my own personal touch."

Ms. Yoo holds up the jacket she's sewing. "Same here," she says. "This pattern called for a zipper. But I decided to replace it. I wanted to show off some of the antique buttons in my collection."

Mr. Hart nods. "Every time I make a new shirt, I have to widen the collar so that it doesn't feel so tight around my neck."

Tía Abuela gave me the sewing kit because of my careful attention to detail. Because I always follow directions. Now the sewists are telling me they *ignore* the instructions. *On purpose?*

I don't realize my shoulders are so tight until Josefina pats them. "Who knows? You might discover you actually like breaking the rules," she says.

I doubt it.

"And I have the perfect pattern for you to practice with," Josefina continues.

It's the second surprise of the afternoon. I have

never sewn with a pattern before! I have never sewn anything more complicated than straight stitches. That can be a little boring, but Josefina insisted that I learn the basics first. I really *must* be making progress.

I follow her to a desk in the corner of the room. She opens a drawer.

"I found this pattern in a box of donations someone brought to the library," she tells me, pulling out a paper envelope. "I knew it was just right for you."

I take the envelope from Josefina's hands and study it. The picture on the front shows two kids modeling the same vest, but in different colors.

"This is a pattern for beginners," Josefina explains. "It only has three pieces."

For beginners. Of course. I begin to frown, but Josefina goes on. "It might look very simple, but that means you can personalize it however you like. Make it your own! Be creative!"

While Josefina clears off a space for me at the cutting table, I dig through the big bin of scrap fabric that she always brings to Stitch and Share. It takes a while to find something, but I finally choose a leopard print that reminds me of something Tía Abuela would wear. I spread it out on the table. "Be creative," I tell myself.

The only problem is, I've never ignored the instructions before. Not on purpose, anyway. I'm not even sure I understand what Josefina meant when she told me to make it my own. For now, I decide to start the way she did, tracing the pattern onto the fabric with a chalk pencil. Maybe some good ideas will come to me while I work.

As I trace, I start humming Tía Abuela's song, the one Banda La Chispa will perform in the talent show—if we get the chance, that is.

Mr. Hart sighs and lets the pajama bottoms he's

working on fall to his lap. "It's been ages since I've heard that song."

Oops. I set down the chalk pencil. "Sorry," I say, "I didn't mean to hum so loudly."

Señora Garcia, one of the newest sewists in our group, shakes her head. "Don't apologize," she says as she sticks a pin into the tomato-shaped pincushion she wears around her wrist. "That song is my favorite."

"And no one could sing it like La Chispa," Mrs. Glass adds.

I swallow hard, wondering if she's right. *From now on, I'll only hum in my head*, I think, turning back to the pattern.

"You know," Josefina says, "we might be able to hear La Chispa sing it. I think we have a recording in the library. One second."

Josefina leaves the community room, and

eighty-seven seconds later (not that I'm counting) comes back with a CD from the music collection. She's also carrying a CD player, which she sets on top of the desk and plugs into the wall. She pops open the top and drops the CD inside.

Everyone stops when she presses play. Tía Abuela's voice pours through the speakers, as silky as the piece of fabric I'm working on. Mr. Hart closes his eyes. Señora Garcia sways in her chair. Then, when Tía Abuela gets to the big chorus, Mr. Hart starts singing too. Soon the whole room is singing. Even Anthony Becerra, the only other kid in Stitch and Share. Even *me*.

I wish Banda La Chispa could play exactly like this.

Maybe we can!

I have the most amazing idea.

"Señora Josefina, when Stitch and Share is over,

• OFF-KEY •

do you think I can borrow that CD?" I ask. "I want my friends to hear it."

If we can follow the recording exactly—the same way I'm trying to follow the lines of this sewing pattern—maybe we can get the song just right.

"Por supuesto, Catalina," Josefina agrees. "We can lend you the CD player too."

· CHAPTER 4 ·

Just Right

The last notes of the song begin to fade. When Tía Abuela's voice is barely a whisper, I look up at the rest of the band.

It's after school on Tuesday, and we're in Pablo's garage. We've agreed to meet for an hour after school each day to rehearse before Friday's auditions.

"Should we listen to it one more time?" I ask. "To make sure we have the notes exactly right?"

Soledad groans. "Catalina," she says, putting her

hand over mine before I can press the play button again. "We've already listened to it *six* times in a row. Can't we just practice the song now?"

Ruthie taps her drumsticks together. "Yeah, Cat, my mom is going to pick me up any minute. I have to get to soccer."

I turn to Pablo.

I might be La Chispa's grand-niece, but Pablo is her number one fan. He knows all of Tía Abuela's roles and has even memorized her most famous lines. Every time he sees her in person, he asks her to sign his autograph book. (She always does.) Disappointing La Chispa—getting her song wrong—is the last thing he'd want to do. I know he'll say we should listen to the recording again.

Instead Pablo folds his arms over his chest. "They never rehearse like this on *Allegro Academy*."

Soledad wrinkles her nose. "What's that?"

Pablo's eyes sparkle. Uh-oh. I know what's coming.

"You've never heard of *Allegro Academy*?" he asks, pressing his hand over his heart as if he is shocked by what she said. "It used to be my mom's favorite telenovela when she was a teenager. We've been watching it together. It's all about the students at a special high school for pop stars and—"

I clear my throat to get their attention. Pablo loves watching telenovelas—the Spanish-language TV shows, full of drama—that Tía Abuela used to star in. He could talk about his latest favorite all afternoon. We don't have time for that.

"Maybe you're right," I say. "We're ready to sing. Let's take it from the top."

Pablo huffs and steps back behind his keyboard. Ruthie sits up straighter at her drum set. I pick up my tambourine.

Once we're all settled, Soledad counts off.

We begin to play.

At first I think it's our best version yet. Listening to Tía Abuela's recording has paid off. Ruthie's beat is strong and steady. Pablo's notes sound like the ones the band played on the CD. When Soledad starts singing, her voice is fierce and fiery, exactly like Tía Abuela's. I shake my tambourine and wait to join in during the chorus.

But then, right as the first verse is about to end, Soledad changes one of the words!

I let the tambourine fall to my side. I look over my shoulder at Ruthie. She doesn't seem to have noticed. I look the other way, at Pablo. He's still playing the keyboard and bopping his head along to the rhythm. I try to ignore what I've just heard. *It's okay if we're not perfect yet*, I tell myself. *We still have a few more days to get it right.*

But it's no use. Soledad's slip-up is just too distracting.

"Wait!" I yell.

The notes all clang together, sour and awful, as the music crashes to a stop.

Pablo freezes with his fingers hovering above the keys.

Ruthie holds her drumsticks in the air.

Soledad strums one more angry chord on her guitar. "Why'd you do that?" she asks. "We sounded great!"

Maybe she doesn't realize she messed up. But that's hard to believe, especially after we listened to the song so many times.

I lower my voice. I don't want to make Soledad feel bad. "You sang the wrong word," I whisper.

"I didn't sing the wrong word!" Soledad shouts back.

At least I *tried* not to call too much attention to it.

"Are you sure, Cat?" Ruthie asks. "I didn't hear anything wrong."

Of course I'm sure. I memorized all the lyrics. I turn to Pablo again. He *must* have heard it too. His attention to detail is almost as sharp as mine. But Pablo doesn't back me up.

I sigh. "At the end of the first verse," I explain. "You made a mistake. It's supposed to be 'maleta,' and you said 'paleta.' They mean completely different things."

"Maleta" means "suitcase"—I know because I looked it up last night. And a paleta is a special kind of frozen fruit bar. I know because the strawberry ones are my favorite summer treat.

"It wasn't a mistake," Soledad says. "I did it on purpose. I thought it sounded better that way."

How could anything sound better than the *right* way?

But I take a deep breath before I say anything

else. I don't want Soledad to feel discouraged.

"Your voice sounded wonderful," I tell her finally. I really mean it too. "Especially at the beginning. But let's try practicing with the correct words. After all, we want to make sure we get a spot in the talent show, don't we?"

They all nod.

"Fine," Soledad says. "Let's try it again."

We take it from the top. This time, I count off, and when we get to the end of the verse, and Soledad sings the correct words, I look back at her and wink.

But just as I do, I notice that Pablo has changed the keyboard notes. They don't sound bad. Just . . . different.

"Wait!" I say again. This time I'm so frustrated that my tambourine slips from my fingers. It clatters to the ground.

"What now?" Soledad demands, her hand on

her hip. "I sang all the right words. Exactly like La Chispa. Exactly like you wanted me to."

It's true. She did. "You were *perfect*," I reassure Soledad. I turn around to face Pablo. "But you . . ."

"I thought it would sound more interesting if I changed the notes a little bit," Pablo explains. "If I played in harmony with Soledad."

Ruthie nods. "I loved it!"

"I got the idea from *Allegro Academy*," Pablo continues. "The characters are always trying to stand out from the crowd."

I try to stay patient, but we are running out of time. Pablo, more than anyone else, should know how important it is to get this song just right.

"But, Pablo," I say, "this isn't *Allegro Academy*." I pick up my tambourine and walk over to the CD player. "Let's listen to the real version again. Just a few more times."

· CHAPTER 5 ·

Extra Help

That night, I lie in bed with my three plush kittens lined up, shortest to tallest, beside my pillow, just the way I like them. While Coco tosses and turns on the top bunk, I think about what Tía Abuela wrote to me in her note. Banda La Chispa seems to be getting better every time we play the song. But singing all afternoon hasn't chased my worries away. In fact, it might have given me new ones.

I am pretty much sure of it: the band is going to

need a little extra help getting into the talent show. *Magical* help.

Finally Coco's breathing turns into a soft snore. Now that she is in a deep sleep, I roll out of bed and sneak to my closet. I stand on tiptoe to reach the highest shelf, where I've hidden the magical sewing kit. When my hand lands on the soft velvet pouch, a jolt shoots up my fingers, like when Coco and I shuffle across the carpet in socks and try to shock each other.

I take the sewing kit down, flip on the closet light, and then sit on the floor. There's plenty of space to work because I always keep my closet so tidy. Not like Coco's. If Mami and Papi walk by, they'll just think I'm up reading past my bedtime. They'll never guess the truth—that I'm sewing up a batch of magical disguises.

Still, I'd better hurry.

I unzip my backpack and take out the vest pattern Josefina the Librarian lent me. Then I find the big piece of purple fabric inside the box Tía Abuela sent. There should be enough to make a vest for each of the band members. And if I use the magical needle and thread, anyone who sees us wearing them will think we're *major* musicians, exactly like the ones on the recording!

Maybe Pablo was right all along. We need something to help us stand out from the crowd. I spread the fabric on the floor and start tracing.

For the next two nights, after Coco has gone to bed, I do the same thing. By Friday, I have sewn four matching purple vests, one for each of us. I'm a little tired, but it was worth it.

I wait until after school on Friday, right before the auditions, to surprise the rest of the band with our new uniforms. Soledad, Ruthie, and Pablo are already lined up inside the auditorium, waiting for our turn to perform.

Ruthie picks at her nail polish. "I'm not used to drumming in front of so many people," she says, her eyes darting around the crowded room. "What if I mess up?"

Soledad pats her back. "Don't worry," she says.

"We're going to do an amazing job. We've been practicing all week."

Now is the perfect moment to show them, to unveil the little bit of magic that will guarantee that the crowd loves us—and the judges too.

"And if all that practice wasn't enough," I say, whipping a gift box from behind my back. "We have these to help us!"

I lift open the lid. Inside are four purple vests, sewn together with shimmering silver thread.

Soledad peers into the box. She pulls out one of the vests and holds it in front of her face, pinching it between her thumb and index finger like it's one of Carlos's dirty diapers.

"What's this for?" she asks.

I hold out the box to Pablo and then to Ruthie. They each take a vest. "Band uniforms, of course,"

I say. "I made them myself. Not only will we *sound* perfect, but we'll *look* perfect too. Like a real band." I don't tell them about the magic. "Quick, put them on."

Soledad frowns and tries to hand the vest back to me. "They're really nice, Cat," she says. "But I was hoping to wear something brighter. Something that will grab everyone's attention when we're onstage. Like this." She reaches into her backpack and pulls out a feathered boa. She wraps it around her neck. Pink and orange feathers flutter to the floor. "Do you like it?" she asks, twirling.

Before I can answer, Ruthie takes a red silk rose out of her pocket. "My grandma gave it to me," she says, gently cradling the flower in her palm. "I like to wear it when I have a test, or anytime I need some extra luck. I could pin it to the vest, though."

I shake my head. "But then we wouldn't match." It would ruin the whole effect.

"Pablo?" I ask. "What do you think?" Surely he'll understand how important this is to me.

"Actually, Catalina," he says, shifting from one foot to the other, "I was going to wear this tie—it's like the one the characters wear in *Allegro Academy*. I don't think I can wear it with your vest. The colors will clash."

He's right about that.

Just then the loudspeaker crackles. "Banda La Chispa, it's your turn to audition," Mr. Stevens, the music teacher, says. "Please make your way to the stage."

It's our turn, and I'm out of time! Somehow I need to get my bandmates to put on the vests. But how can I convince them without revealing the secret of the magic sewing kit?

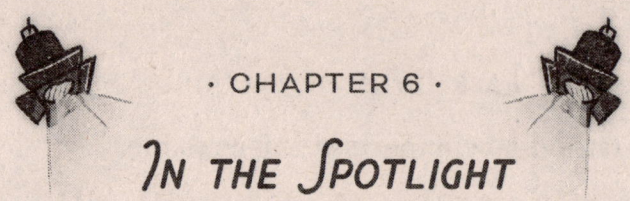

· CHAPTER 6 ·

In the Spotlight

"Please wear them?" I beg. "We don't want all our practice to go to waste, all because we don't look perfectly put together."

No one moves. They just blink back at me.

"Do it for me?" I ask. "Do it for . . . La Chispa."

Pablo's shoulders slump. I knew he wouldn't be able to turn me down after I mentioned Tía Abuela. Once he changes his mind, Ruthie and Soledad do as well.

"Are you happy now?" Soledad asks.

"Very," I say. And soon the rest of the band will be too. I know it. But there isn't time to waste. Mr. Stevens's voice crackles through the speaker again.

"Banda La Chispa?"

"Vamos!" I yell. "Let's go. We can't be late!"

I race up the steps to the stage. The rest of the

band scrambles behind me as they try to put on their new vests.

We finally get into position. All the other groups waiting to audition stop what they're doing to watch. I glance down at the vest. The purple fabric gleams. The silver thread glitters.

"Look, it's Banda La Chispa!" someone calls out.

Someone else whistles.

The judges lean forward in their seats.

The disguises are working! Everyone thinks we're a real band!

Ruthie shrinks behind her drums. "Why are they staring at us like that?" she asks. "Why are they already cheering?"

I grin. "It's because they know we're going to be absolutely . . . magical!" I reply.

This must be what Tía Abuela feels like every time she stands in the spotlight, ready to perform.

This must be what she meant when she said that singing chases your worries away.

I gather the band into one last huddle.

"Let's play it exactly the way we practiced," I remind them. "The way it sounds in the recording." I turn to Ruthie. "You'll make sure to keep the beat strong and steady?"

She nods. "Y-yup," she says, before her eyes flutter back to the crowd gathering in front of the stage.

"And, Pablo," I say next, "you'll play the chords the way they were written? No special harmonies this time?"

"If you say so," he answers glumly. Then he steps out of the huddle and goes to his keyboard. I'm sure Pablo will cheer up once we earn our spot in the talent show.

Last, I come to Soledad. The crowd is chanting, "Canten! Canten!" Sing! Sing!

"And you'll say the correct words?" I ask her. "Did you remember to write them out three times last night? That always helps me memorize."

Soledad huffs. "Maybe *you'd* better sing, Catalina. That way you'll know that everything is exactly the way *you* want it." She grabs the microphone stand and moves it to my spot between Pablo and Ruthie.

I can't tell if Soledad is angry or nervous. Either way, it isn't such a bad idea. After all, I have been listening to the song, note by note, measure by measure, all week long. I know it by heart.

"You're right," I say. "I will!"

By now the cheering is so loud that we almost can't hear one another. I rattle the tambourine to get the band's attention. Then I count us off. "Uno, dos, tres, cuatro!"

Ruthie's drumming keeps us all moving at an even tempo. Pablo's keyboard notes blend perfectly with Soledad's guitar chords. The music swirls around my head as I shake my tambourine along with the beat. When I throw back my head and begin to sing, I pretend I am La Chispa. I wish she could see me now. But after this audition, I'm sure she'll get a chance to see me at the talent show next week.

We make it to the end of the song without missing a single note. I know because I've been paying attention to each and every one of them. My plan worked! We sounded just like Tía Abuela's famous recording. I'll have to tell Josefina the Librarian. Sometimes it's a good thing to follow the pattern. In sewing *and* in singing.

The crowd cheers again as we bow. I wave and

blow kisses, the same way I've seen Tía Abuela do when she finishes a spectacular performance. But then, when I turn to see if the rest of the band is enjoying the attention as much as I am, I realize they aren't there anymore. I'm all alone onstage. *They probably wanted to rush home to tell their families what a great job we all did*, I think. But even I don't quite believe it.

· CHAPTER 7 ·

Solo

The hallway is already crowded when I get to Valle Grande Elementary early on Monday morning. It seems like the whole school is crammed outside the music room, where the talent show list is posted on the wall.

I nudge my way through, wishing I had a snake disfraz to help me get to the list faster. The other kids would step aside if they thought I was a snake.

I make a mental note to add boa constrictor to my costume wish list.

When I get to the front of the crowd, I scan the list, looking for "Banda La Chispa." I don't have to look for long. We're first on the lineup! We made it!

I can't wait to find Pablo, Soledad, and Ruthie so we can celebrate. Tía Abuela is going to hear us perform her song! And the best part is, we've already spent so much time practicing that it's sure to be a *perfect* performance. All we have to do is repeat what we did for the audition.

But my friends aren't in any of the usual places. Not swinging on the playground, not grabbing a breakfast sandwich in the cafeteria, not even reading in the library. Finally I have to head to the third-grade classroom. The bell is about to ring, and I am always on time.

To my surprise, Pablo, Soledad, and Ruthie are already there, slouching in their seats.

They must not have heard. Now I can be the one to share the amazing news.

"We made it!" I shout, breaking a major classroom rule for maybe the first time ever. But I have a very good reason. "We're in the talent show!"

I thought they would cheer. Or smile. Or even lift their eyes off the ground.

But they don't.

"Yeah," Pablo says, and shrugs, "we know."

If they know, they shouldn't look so disappointed. Maybe they're tired. I know I had a hard time falling asleep last night. My thoughts raced as I wondered if we'd made the show and worried that maybe we hadn't.

They can't still be angry over the vests, can they? Not after our performance went so well.

"If you already know, then why aren't you happy?" I ask.

Soledad looks up. She narrows her eyes behind her round glasses. For the first time, I notice the purple vest hanging over the back of her chair. *She should have left the vest at home*, I think. There's no telling what might stain it at school. A pen could leak. Chocolate milk could spill. You could slip and fall on the grass. And we want our costumes to look fresh and clean at the talent show on Friday.

But I don't mention it. I almost couldn't resist wearing my vest to school either.

"We are not performing," Soledad says.

I'm so surprised that I leap backward. "Of course we are," I argue. "You just heard me, didn't you? We got in."

Soledad shakes her head. "I know we got in, but we're quitting the band. It was fun at the beginning, when we were all trying our best and trying new things," she says. "But ever since we started copying the original—singing it over and over again, exactly the same way—it's gotten kind of . . . boring."

"Not just *kind of*," Pablo mutters.

Soledad takes the vest from the back of her

chair and holds it out to me. "Here," she says. "I don't think I was cut out to be in Banda La Chispa after all."

I take the vest, only because I'm worried that if I don't, it'll fall to the floor.

"But what about everyone cheering for us?" I ask. "They wouldn't have cheered like that if we hadn't done a great job."

Next Ruthie holds out her vest. "It was awful," she confesses, her voice shaky. "I was so worried I was going to mess up that my stomach hurt all day. I'm leaving the band too."

I didn't know she felt that way. I can't stand messing up either—that's why I wanted to practice so much.

"Well," I say, walking toward Pablo's desk, "I guess it's just you and me. But don't worry. Tía Abuela is going to love us, even if we're not playing

with the whole band anymore."

Pablo sighs. He unzips his book bag and takes out his vest, folded into a neat purple square.

"I'm not performing either," he says softly, setting the vest on the corner of my desk.

"But why?" I ask, taking another step toward him. "Don't you want to perform for La Chispa? Isn't this your dream?"

Pablo keeps staring down at the floor without saying anything. Then the tips of his ears begin to turn pink. Next the color spreads to his cheeks. These are not good signs.

"It was my dream until you took over," Pablo says, turning to me. "I had some good ideas, but you wouldn't even listen to any of them. You were so focused on making everything perfect that you didn't let us make it our own. La Chispa would never have done that."

That's when the bell rings. Suddenly I am a solo act.

· CHAPTER 8 ·

Incognito

I walk home by myself that afternoon. I should be walking to Pablo's house. The band agreed that if we made it into the talent show, we'd keep meeting in his garage to practice. But now there's no band. There's only me.

Even though it isn't very cold outside, I take my favorite gray sweatshirt out of my backpack. I always carry it with me, but it wasn't always my favorite. Especially after Tía Abuela sewed kitten ears onto the hood. (No one *ever* listens when I tell them I'm getting too old for all the kitten stuff.)

But then I realized that Tía Abuela had sewn the ears on with magic. That means the sweatshirt is more than a sweatshirt. It's also a disfraz. Which makes it just what I need. Right now I feel like hiding, and going incognito is the next-best thing.

I push my arms through the sweatshirt sleeves and pull the zipper up to my neck.

Next I look around to make sure no one is watching. I pull the hood over my head, and a shiver runs up my spine. When I look down at my shadow on the sidewalk, I don't see the shadow of a girl anymore. I see the shadow of a cat.

As I dart behind cars and hedges and garbage cans, I wonder how I'm going to pull off the talent show performance on my own. My bandmates—*former* bandmates, that is—are being so unfair.

They wanted to make it into the talent show, didn't they? Thanks to me, we did.

When I'm almost back to my house, I hear the rumble of skateboard wheels rolling over the street. Coco.

It's lucky I'm incognito. I'm not ready to tell my family what happened with the band. They'll find out soon enough when I'm the only one onstage at the talent show on Friday.

I drop my backpack and crouch behind the neighbor's rosebush to watch.

Coco is working on her kick flip. I know because I've seen her practice the trick on the street in front of our house every weekend for the past month. Over and over and over.

She must be getting ready for Tía Abuela's visit too. This surprises me because Coco doesn't always appreciate good preparation. You should see her

rushing to pack up her school supplies at the very last minute every morning.

But as I watch, I realize that Coco isn't doing the same trick over and over. She's doing *almost* the same trick, but a little different each time. Once, she lands with her legs crossed, one over the other. The next time, she lands on one foot.

Not Coco too! "Why don't you just do it the *right* way?" I shout as she prepares to do the trick again. Only, the words don't come out in my voice. They come out like the yowl of an angry cat.

Whoops. I forgot all about the disfraz. I try to scamper away before Coco sees me. But it's too late. She hops off her skateboard.

"Hey," she says, turning around. "You ruined my trick."

I want to tell her that *she* ruined it herself with all those changes. But I don't dare move a whisker.

Coco squints at me. "You look sorta familiar," she says. "You must be that cat Mami is always complaining about. The one who hangs around our house like she lives there."

I *do* live there. But Coco doesn't know that. I skitter backward and dive behind the roses.

I'm crawling away when a thorn pricks my wrist. "Ouch!" I yelp.

It comes out in my real voice. Oh no! I touch the top of my head and realize I'm not wearing the hood anymore. It must have snagged on one of the thorns. I am no longer incognito.

"Is that . . . Cat?"

Slowly I stand. Coco watches with her eyes wide, her mouth hanging open. "Have you been hiding in the bushes the whole time?"

"I . . . um . . . ," I sputter, trying to think of an explanation. "Yes! I was watching you skate, but I didn't want to disturb you." I brush some rose petals off my leggings.

Coco comes closer, like she doesn't believe me. She peers into the bush. "There was a cat just now—right here, right where you're standing," she says. "Did you see her?"

I look behind me, pretending to search for the mystery cat that I know isn't there anymore.

"Maaaybe," I answer, "but she must have run away." I change the subject. "What are you working on? I thought you already perfected your kick flip."

Coco tightens the strap of her helmet under her chin. "I did," she says. "But now I want to put my own personal stamp on it. I've always wanted to have a trick named after me. Watch this."

Coco jumps back onto her skateboard, and I sit on the curb to watch. She pushes off. Once she's rolling, she steps down hard on the back of the board to pop it into the air. Then she flicks the board with her front foot so it spirals under her feet. When she comes back

down, she lands on the back two wheels, the skateboard's nose pointing in the air.

It was so exciting, I don't even mind that she didn't do the trick the right way. "Bravo!" I say, and clap.

Coco unfastens her helmet. "What did you think of that one?" she asks. "Tell me the truth."

I tap my finger against my lips. "Hmmm . . . I think you should call it the Coco-kick."

· CHAPTER 9 ·

Sew Busy

The longer I watch Coco trying out new ways to land her skateboard trick, the more I understand why Pablo, Soledad, and Ruthie were so frustrated with me. They wanted to sing Tía Abuela's song, but they didn't want to sing it just like Tía Abuela. They wanted to make it their own. They wanted the song to fit their styles the same way Josefina the Librarian wanted the dress she was sewing to fit her style.

As soon as Coco and I get home, I race upstairs to

our bedroom. I open my sketchbook to a fresh page and take my colored pencils out of their drawer. It's a good thing I always keep them sharpened. I get to work, and when I'm finished, there's barely enough time to make it to Stitch and Share.

"I was getting worried," Josefina the Librarian says as I burst through the doors. "You're usually here so early."

Early to Josefina is right on time for me.

I look around the room as I catch my breath. For once, some of the other sewists have arrived before me. That's a good thing. At Stitch and Share, there's always someone to help if you need it. And I need plenty.

Josefina notices the bundles of fabric I'm carrying under one arm and the drawings I'm holding in the other.

She claps.

"Oh good!" she says. "It looks like you've come up with an idea for the vest you started last week. I knew you'd think of a way to make it your own."

I drop my supplies onto the cutting table that's still set up in the center of the room. "I haven't thought of *one* idea," I tell her. "I thought of *three*."

I wave the other sewists over. "My friends and I are supposed to perform in the school talent show on Friday," I explain. "At first I thought we should all match, but that didn't work very well. Now I want to try something *different*."

I spread out my drawings. Three different vests to match three different personalities. "But I'm going to need some help," I finish.

Josefina the Librarian picks up one of the sketches. "You didn't just make the pattern your own," she says. "You made your own patterns!"

I hold my breath, hoping Josefina doesn't mind

that I ignored the instructions completely. I'm nervous that she'll say I need more practice before I can sew these new vests.

Instead she says, "Excelente, Catalina! These

are even better than the original. I'll help you. Does anyone else have time to set aside their projects to work on Catalina's costumes?"

Señora Garcia takes the drawing I made of Soledad's vest. She squints at it. "Sequins can be very tricky to sew with," she says. "Luckily, I just sewed a mermaid costume for my neighbor that was covered in sequins. I can show you all the tricks I learned."

Mr. Hart picks up the sketch of Ruthie's vest. "This one has the same shape as a fishing vest I made not too long ago," he says. "I can help you make a pattern piece." He gets up off his folding chair and makes his way to the desk in the corner to find some drawing paper.

"And I have some buttons in my collection that will match perfectly," Ms. Yoo says. "I'll show you how to stitch them on so they never come loose."

For the rest of Stitch and Share, I flutter from chair to chair, almost as if I am still wearing my butterfly wings. When Anthony and Mrs. Glass arrive, they join other sewists in helping me bring my costume designs to life—*without* any magic.

By the time the session is over, the new vests are ready and even better than I imagined. I pack them up with the rest of my sewing supplies, careful not to let them wrinkle.

"Don't forget this one," Josefina the Librarian says. She holds up a leopard-print vest. It's the one I started last week at Stitch and Share, when I didn't know how to make a pattern my own. I had forgotten all about it.

"I noticed you hadn't designed a costume for yourself, so I thought I'd finish this one for you," she says. I was so busy—more like *sew* busy—that I didn't even notice her working on it.

"And I added something special, just for you," Josefina continues.

"Pockets?" I ask. Pockets would be very useful. I could keep a spare needle and thread inside, just in case of sewing emergencies.

"No," Josefina says, turning the vest around to reveal . . . a tail. "Isn't it *purr*-fect?"

I sigh. More kittens. Of course.

Still, I take the vest and fold it with the others. "Gracias!" I shout as I wave goodbye.

· CHAPTER 10 ·

Even Better

It's Friday, and Banda La Chispa is still on the talent show lineup. I just hope there's still a band.

The talent show is set to begin right after lunch. I watch from backstage with the rest of the performers as kids begin to fill the auditorium, kindergartners in the first rows and sixth graders near the back. Behind them, teachers set out chairs for parents and other relatives. Soon Tía Abuela will be sitting in one of them. She said she'd be coming straight from the airport. I hope she won't be too disappointed when she doesn't see me onstage.

Because if my plan works out, I might not be singing.

Finally the third graders file into the auditorium. Mr. Stevens is so busy backstage that he doesn't notice me step out from behind the curtain to find Pablo, Soledad, and Ruthie in the audience. He doesn't notice the box I'm carrying either.

"Shouldn't you be getting ready to sing?" Pablo asks when I make my way to his seat. He gives his watch a nervous glance. "There's only a few more minutes before the show starts. Aren't you worried you'll be late?"

I'm worried *he'll* be late. Pablo and the rest of the band. "That's why I'm here," I say. "I want the band—all of you—to sing the song. I'm sorry I didn't listen to your ideas before. I was afraid that if we changed the song, we'd ruin it. But now I understand that you were trying to make it even better."

Soledad points to the box tucked under my arm. "What's that?" She wrinkles her nose. "Not the vests again?"

"Not exactly," I say, taking off the lid. "I changed the pattern. The vests don't match anymore. But this time, they might actually fit you."

The first vest goes to Ruthie. It's made out of the zebra-print fabric that Tía Abuela sent from Colombia. "I know you love animal accessories," I explain. "And I thought your grandma's red rose would look great with the black-and-white fabric."

Ruthie hugs the vest to her chest. "I love it!" she exclaims.

The next one is for Soledad. It's covered in pink and orange sequins that shimmer in the light. "You told me you wanted to stand out onstage," I say.

"Well, no one will be able to miss you in this. It even goes with your feather boa."

Soledad grabs the vest before I've even finished explaining. "It's perfect!" she says, holding it up in front of her face. The auditorium lights bounce off the sequins and dance in her glasses.

I catch Pablo trying to sneak a peek at the box out of the corner of his eye.

Carefully I remove his vest. "And I made this one especially for you, Pablo," I say.

When he sees the vest, his eyes widen. It's red with blue trim.

"This looks exactly like the uniform on—"

"Allegro Academy!" I finish the sentence for him. "I know! Josefina the Librarian searched for pictures online so I could get the details just right." I frown. "I didn't have enough time to make the tie, though."

Pablo smiles. He reaches into his pocket and

pulls out a striped tie. "I always come prepared," he replies.

There's one more thing to say, and I'd better hurry because the show is about to start. The principal is already at the front of the stage, trying to settle everyone down.

"You don't have to wear the vests," I whisper. "But I wanted you to know that I really *was* listening. Your ideas will make Tía Abuela's song better than ever. You should perform it instead of me."

My eyes begin to sting. I blink to stop myself from crying. I don't want to miss my chance in the spotlight—my chance to impress Tía Abuela—but I know she'll be proud of my progress. And not just in sewing.

"Vamos!" Soledad shouts. I watch her, Pablo, and Ruthie jump from their seats and start making their way backstage. Just as I'm about to slump down into Pablo's empty spot, Soledad pauses and looks over her shoulder.

"Aren't you coming?" she asks. "The show's going to start any second. And you know what Pablo says. 'Late is late.'"

"Really?" I almost can't believe it. They were so upset with me after the audition.

Pablo stops too. "Of course," he says. "If you hadn't made us practice so much, we wouldn't sound as good as we do."

"But what will you wear?" Ruthie asks. "We all have these great new costumes, and you don't have anything."

Luckily, there's one more vest in the box. "Don't worry," I say, putting on the leopard-print vest that Josefina the Librarian made me. I brought it just in case. "I have something *purr-fect*."

· CHAPTER 11 ·

A Perfect Performance

A few of us peek out from behind the curtains as Aaron Chu finishes his magic act with a swish of his cape. This time, a bouquet of daisies pops up out of his hat. We cheer along with the audience.

When Aaron finishes his bows, Esme and Jazmín walk onstage together. They have matching ribbons in their braids. As they dance, their swirling blue skirts look like flowers opening and closing. The sound of their stamping boots echoes through the auditorium.

• OFF-KEY •

They don't miss a step.

We clap again as their song ends. "It's almost time," I whisper to myself.

"Next up," Mr. Stevens announces, "is Banda La Chispa."

Pablo, Soledad, Ruthie, and I take the stage. As Mr. Stevens helps Pablo set up his keyboard, I peer out into the audience. Mami and Papi smile back at me. Baby Carlos laughs on Mami's lap. But the chair next to Papi's is empty. Tía Abuela hasn't arrived yet. After so much work, I hope she doesn't miss our performance!

I help Soledad adjust her microphone. But before we're finished, she says, "Wait. What if we *all* sing?"

The rest of the band looks at me. "Well . . ." I hesitate.

We've never practiced singing the whole song together. And it's definitely not the way Tía Abuela performed it. I'm not sure this is the right time to change things up. But then, I remind myself, sometimes experimenting with new ideas can be fun.

"Let's do it!" I say.

Quickly we move the microphone stand to the middle of the stage, where it will pick up all of our voices.

Finally it's time to sing.

My heart thumps as Soledad begins counting off.

"Uno, dos—"

Just then I hear a *click-clack, click-clack* on the auditorium floor. I know who it is without even looking.

Tía Abuela. She is wearing her favorite high-heeled boots and her cat-eye sunglasses with rhinestones in the corners. She made it!

"¡Perdón!" she says as she squeezes her way

• OFF-KEY •

across the row to the empty seat next to Papi. "I'm sorry I'm late."

Tía Abuela isn't late, though. She is right on time.

I wave, and she waves back. She lowers her sunglasses and gives the band a wink.

That's our signal. "Vamos!" I yell.

Ruthie's drumbeat is faster than ever, and I laugh, trying to match the rhythm with my tambourine.

Pablo tries out new harmonies on the keyboard, and Soledad changes a few more words. Sometimes we aren't singing the same lyrics, but we're all singing from the heart.

I don't know if Tía Abuela will like it, but I know we're having fun.

The whole audience whistles and claps along—and we didn't even need magical disguises.

When Soledad strums her last chord, Tía Abuela is the first to leap to her feet.

"Bravo!" she cries. The rest of the audience jumps up and joins her in cheering. Banda La Chispa bows—together this time. Soledad and Pablo blow kisses at the audience.

• OFF-KEY •

At the end of the show, after helping to pack up the instruments, I try to find Tía Abuela. As usual, a crowd of fans has swarmed her. As usual, Pablo is at the center of it, asking for yet *another* autograph.

When she finishes signing, Tía Abuela wraps her arms around me and squeezes tight.

"That was unlike anything I have ever heard before," she tells me.

In other words, it was *perfect*.

Turn the page for a sneak peek at Catalina's next magical adventure!

Skateboard Slump

I sharpen my colored pencils into perfect points and arrange them in rainbow order, just like I do every Saturday morning. That way, they are always ready when I need them.

I'm working at the kitchen table so that my baby brother, Carlos, who is rolling toy trucks on the floor with Papi, doesn't disturb me. You can't be too careful with Carlos around. I've found his tiny teeth marks on my school supplies before!

Right as I am about to place parakeet green next to lemon yellow, my big sister stomps past and bumps into my shoulder. She knocks my hand into the box of colored pencils and sends them tumbling to the floor.

"Coco!" I yell. She has never appreciated the importance of a good organization system. But that doesn't mean she can ruin mine. "Be careful!"

"Sorry, Cat," Coco says. She is carrying her skateboard and sets it down to help me pick up the pencils. At first, I try to keep them all in rainbow order. But then Carlos comes crawling toward us, drool dribbling off his bottom lip. I scramble to collect the rest of them as quickly as I can.

"What's the rush, Coco?" Papi asks as he scoops Carlos back onto his lap. Mami won't be back from her shift at the nursing home until dinnertime.

Coco puts the candy-apple-red pencil next to the midnight-blue one, nowhere near where it belongs.

"Can I go out skateboarding?" she asks.

She is already wearing her helmet and pads, and her old flannel shirt is balled up under her arm. It's going to be a wrinkled mess when she puts it on.

"Have you made your bed?" Papi asks.

"Of course!" Coco replies.

"Ha!" I bark.

Coco's idea of making the bed is piling her pajamas, sheets, and blanket on top of it in a lumpy heap. I should know. I have to share a room with her.

But Papi seems convinced. "Have fun," he says. "Be careful."

I take the red pencil out of the box and put it back where it's supposed to be—next to tangerine orange. "Wait up," I say. "Give me a minute to put the rest of these pencils away, and I'll come too."

Coco has been helping me learn to skateboard. Since all my chores are finished—including some that Mami and Papi didn't even think of—I can go with her to learn some new tricks.

"No!" Coco says.

"No?" I repeat. Coco doesn't always let me borrow her board, but she's never said I couldn't come with her to skate.

"I really need to concentrate this time," she says. "I need to be alone."

I turn to Papi. "Por favor. Pleeeeeeeease," I say, begging in two languages.

It doesn't work.

"Sorry, Kitty-Cat," Papi says. "Sounds like Coco needs her space."

Being called "Kitty-Cat" is pretty annoying. I've asked my parents about a zillion times to start using my real name, "Catalina." But even more annoying is not getting to go out with Coco. I grab the pencil box and storm upstairs to our room.

Not that I plan to stay there.

As soon as I hear Coco's skateboard rattle down the sidewalk, I go to my closet. I pick out my favorite sweatshirt. It's gray with kitten ears sewn onto the hood. My tía abuela—her name is "Catalina Castañeda" too—sewed it for me. Normally, I wouldn't wear it. Like I keep telling my Mami and Papi, I'm getting too old for all the kitten stuff. But today the sweatshirt is exactly what I need.

I creep back down the stairs, tiptoe down the hall, and sneak out the side door.

Then, flattening myself against the house so that no one can see, I put on the sweatshirt. I zip it up to my chin. I pull the hood over my head. A shiver runs up my spine. I check my reflection in one of the windows. A gray cat blinks back at me. I am incognito.

Tía Abuela didn't make the sweatshirt with

a regular needle and thread. She used a special sewing kit with the power to create magical disguises. Better yet, she passed the magic on to me!

I trot down the street to find Coco. She might have said I couldn't watch her skateboard, but she didn't say anything about a *cat* watching.

I find Coco at the end of the block. She must really not want anyone to see her.

I can understand why. She's wearing her flannel, but it's way too short, and her elbow pokes out of a hole in the sleeve. I shudder. I wouldn't want to be seen in that thing either.

Then again, Coco doesn't care very much about what anyone else thinks of her clothes. Something else must be bothering her. I step closer and stop to watch under the shade of a blue mailbox.

Coco tightens her helmet. She wipes her palms against her shorts and takes off.

I recognize this move. It's her signature trick, the Coco-kick. She steps down onto the back of the board and launches it into the air. Next she's supposed to flick the board with her toe so it spins underneath her. Instead, she kicks it off to the side and lands on her knees.

Ouch.

She tries an easier trick, one she has landed millions of times. But she just keeps crashing.

"What's going on?" I ask. Only, I'm still incognito and it comes out like a curious purr. Coco lifts her head off the sidewalk where she's still sprawled.

"I was hoping nobody saw that," she said. "But you won't tell, will you?" She sits up and scoots closer to me. "You seem familiar. Have I seen you before?"

I skitter backward.

Coco shakes her head and unbuckles her

helmet. "I need to land the Coco-kick for the Skate Spectacular," she says. "It has to be perfect. But I can't seem to get anything right. I might as well go home."

Home? Uh-oh.

Looking for another great book?
Find it
IN THE MIDDLE.

Fun, fantastic books for kids
in the in-be**TWEEN** age.

IntheMiddleBooks.com

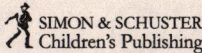 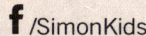 /SimonKids 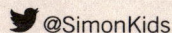 @SimonKids

READ & LEARN
with *simon* kids

Keep your child reading, learning, and having fun with Simon Kids!

A one-stop shop where you can
find downloadable resources, watch interactive author videos, browse books by reading level, and more!

**Visit us at
SimonandSchusterPublishing.com/ReadandLearn/**

And follow us @SimonKids

 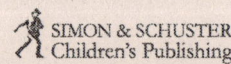 

The New
Friend Fix

DON'T MISS CATALINA'S OTHER MAGICAL ADVENTURES!

Catalina Incognito
Off-Key

BY **Jennifer Torres**

CATALINA INCOGNITO

The New Friend Fix

ILLUSTRATED BY
Gladys Jose

ALADDIN
New York London Toronto Sydney New Delhi

If you purchased this book without a cover, you should be aware that this book is stolen property. It was reported as "unsold and destroyed" to the publisher, and neither the author nor the publisher has received any payment for this "stripped book."

This book is a work of fiction. Any references to historical events, real people, or real places are used fictitiously. Other names, characters, places, and events are products of the author's imagination, and any resemblance to actual events or places or persons, living or dead, is entirely coincidental.

ALADDIN
An imprint of Simon & Schuster Children's Publishing Division
1230 Avenue of the Americas, New York, New York 10020
First Aladdin paperback edition March 2022
Text copyright © 2022 by Jennifer Torres
Illustrations copyright © 2022 by Gladys Jose
Also available in an Aladdin hardcover edition.
All rights reserved, including the right of reproduction in whole or in part in any form.
ALADDIN and related logo are registered trademarks of Simon & Schuster, Inc.
For information about special discounts for bulk purchases, please contact
Simon & Schuster Special Sales at 1-866-506-1949 or business@simonandschuster.com.
The Simon & Schuster Speakers Bureau can bring authors to your live event. For more information or to book an event contact the Simon & Schuster Speakers Bureau at 1-866-248-3049 or visit our website at www.simonspeakers.com.
Designed by Laura Lyn DiSiena
The illustrations for this book were rendered digitally.
The text of this book was set in Century Schoolbook.
Manufactured in the United States of America 0623 OFF
2 4 6 8 10 9 7 5 3
Library of Congress Control Number 2021937747
ISBN 9781534483071 (hc)
ISBN 9781534483064 (pbk)
ISBN 9781534483088 (ebook)

FOR MY GRANDFATHER, VALDEMAR ESPINOZA,
WHO KNOWS THE MAGIC OF A GOOD STORY

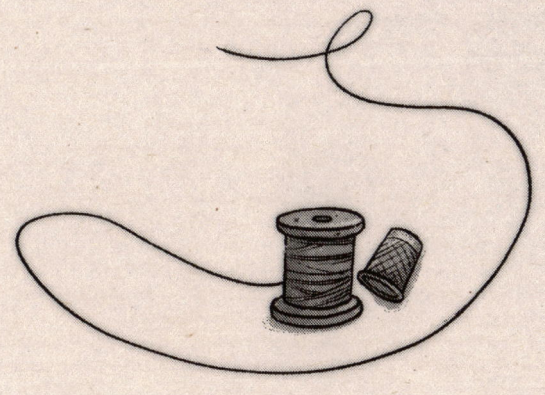

Contents

CHAPTER 1	First Day	1
CHAPTER 2	The New Girl	11
CHAPTER 3	Mean Jazmín	19
CHAPTER 4	Something Magical	27
CHAPTER 5	Stitch and Share	34
CHAPTER 6	Incognito	42
CHAPTER 7	Messy Business	51
CHAPTER 8	Too Much	59
CHAPTER 9	What Really Happened	67
CHAPTER 10	A New Plan	73
CHAPTER 11	Surprise Sewing	81
CHAPTER 12	Right on Time	88

CHAPTER 1

First Day

I have already slurped the last sugary drops of cereal milk off my spoon by the time my big sister, Coco, stumbles to the table.

She yawns and rubs her eyes, then asks, "You're already dressed, Cat?"

"Of course I am." It's the first day of school, after all. Last night I spent two hours organizing my backpack, filling the pouches and pockets with freshly sharpened pencils, never-used erasers, and notebooks with nothing but blank pages inside. Everything is perfectly put together.

Stuffing a backpack with new school supplies is one of my all-time favorite activities. Which means the day before school starts is one of my all-time favorite days of the year.

"But it's so early," Coco whines.

"It's never too early to be prepared," I answer.

Papi sets a bowl of cereal in front of Coco while I carry my empty bowl to the sink.

"Buenos días!" he greets her.

"Ugh," Coco moans.

Baby Carlos, our little brother, bangs his palms against his high-chair tray, and Papi drops a few chunks of strawberry onto it. Carlos picks one up and mashes it in his fist.

Even though his sticky hands can't reach me, I still take a big step backward. Just in case.

Mami walks into the kitchen dressed in purple scrubs, all set for her shift at the nursing home.

"Are you excited to start middle school?" she asks, ruffling Coco's sleep-tangled hair.

Coco shrugs.

No one asks if I'm excited to start third grade. Maybe they think it will be just like any other year. Unlike Coco, I'm not going to a new school. But there will still be a new classroom, a new teacher, and—according to my best friend, and biggest rival, Pablo Blanco—a new kid. He heard all about her because his mom is the room parent.

Just one more reason to get to school early. Then *I'll* get to meet the new girl before anyone else does. Even Pablo.

I check to make sure my double-knotted shoelaces haven't come undone, then swing my backpack over my shoulder.

"See you later!" I announce.

Carlos gurgles and waves his gooey hand. Mami and Papi walk over to hug me goodbye.

"Have a wonderful day, mija," Papi says.

"I can't wait to hear all about it," Mami adds, and kisses my forehead.

"Wait!" Coco's mouth is full of frosted wheat squares. "What's the hurry? Give me a few more minutes, and I'll walk with you. Like always."

My hand hovers over the doorknob. Coco and I used to walk to school together every day. But I never thought she actually *wanted* to.

"But we don't go to the same school anymore, remember?" I say, turning the knob.

"We can walk to the corner at least," Coco persists. "I'll even let you ride my skateboard."

Hmm. Coco has been teaching me to ride her skateboard all summer. But only in front of our house. She's never offered to let me ride it anywhere else before.

Even Mami and Papi are surprised.

"Did you hear that, Kitty-Cat?" Papi asks. "Coco says you can ride her skateboard!"

I am tempted to tell Coco yes.

I am tempted to tell Papi to quit calling me "Kitty-Cat."

But, *no*, I decide. There isn't time. I need to get to school. I only have one chance to be the first person to meet the new girl. Then I'll get to introduce her to everyone else. Maybe our teacher will even pick me to show her around school.

"Thanks anyway, Coco," I say. "Maybe tomorrow."

I am stepping out the door when Coco stops me *again*.

"You're wearing *that*?"

My shoulders drop. I hoped no one would notice.

"Didn't you say you were getting too old for all the kitten stuff?" Coco continues.

Slowly I turn around. Coco is pointing at the gray sweatshirt tied around my waist. Two kitten ears and a diamond-shaped patch of white fur are sewn to the hood.

"At least I don't sleep in it too," I say, pointing back at the old flannel shirt Coco *never* takes off.

Coco straightens the collar. "This shirt is *lucky*."

"Well, this sweatshirt," I answer, "is . . . *special*."

"That's right," Mami says. She wraps her arm around my shoulders and squeezes. "Tía Abuela sewed the ears on herself. And I'm sure Kitty-Cat likes wearing it because she misses Tía Abuela. Isn't that right?"

I nod. Tía Abuela is my great-aunt. Her name is Catalina Castañeda just like mine. She used to be a famous telenovela actress. Ever since she retired, Tía Abuela spends most of her time traveling the world. She doesn't come to our house on the hill in Valle Grande very often, so I *do* miss her.

But that's not the only reason why this sweatshirt is special.

On her last visit Tía Abuela gave me a musty old sewing kit in a red velvet pouch. Inside is a needle and a spool of silvery thread. They don't sew regular clothes, though. They create magical disguises. Like this sweatshirt. As soon as I zip it up and pull on the hood, I'll look exactly like an *actual* cat. Over the summer I even used my disfraz to solve a major mystery. So far I haven't shared the secret of the sewing kit with *anyone*.

Before she left on her latest adventure, Tía Abuela warned me that the magic would only be as strong as my stitches. Since I'm still learning, I haven't been able to sew a new disfraz yet. That's why I'm stuck with this one. Even if I *am* getting too old for all this kitten stuff.

I look down at my watch. "Better go," I say. "You know how I feel about being late."

Mami and Papi shudder. Even Coco stops arguing.

I smile to myself and scamper down the front porch steps and out to the sidewalk. Once I'm a few houses down, where I'm sure my family can't see me, I duck behind a mailbox.

I look left and right to make sure no one is watching. I put on the sweatshirt and zip it to my chin.

Then I lift the hood over my head. A chill runs up my spine.

I stand and glance down at my shadow on the pavement. It's not the shadow of a girl anymore. It's the shadow of a cat.

I am *incognito*.

· CHAPTER 2 ·

The New Girl

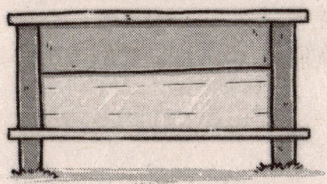

I prowl Valle Grande Elementary School, hoping to catch a glimpse of the new girl before anyone else does.

I dart from behind the drinking fountain to a playground bench. Peering out from underneath, I watch kids pose for pictures next to the school sign. Red and gold balloons bob on either side of it, and black letters on the front spell out "Welcome Back!"

The *B* is a little bit crooked, though. Someone

should have used a ruler! I wish I could ignore it, but I can't. In fact, I am so distracted that I don't notice Mr. Clark, the school custodian, walking toward me with a push broom until he's crouching right in front of my nose.

"You don't belong here," he says gently. "Someone might be allergic."

Uh-oh. I scramble backward, then dash for the school garden.

"Hey, wait!" Mr. Clark calls after me.

I dive between two tomato plants and hide behind a tangle of leaves. Luckily for me, someone drops a thermos full of macaroni and cheese on the ground, and Mr. Clark stops to help clean it.

I let my breath out slowly and shakily. That new

girl better get here soon. I need to change out of this disfraz before the bell rings—and before I get caught.

Finally I spot her: a girl about my age who I've never seen at school before. She has two long braids, round glasses, and a sprinkle of freckles across her nose.

But she isn't alone. She's walking—and talking!—with Jazmín Galindo, another third grader. How could Jazmín have met the new girl first? Even worse, *Pablo* is speeding toward them!

I'm about to leap from the garden box, when I remember I am still incognito. As quickly as I can, I yank off my hood and pat down my hair. When I'm certain no one is looking, I climb out.

By the time I catch up with Jazmín and the new girl, Pablo is already introducing himself. Or, at least he's trying to.

• Jennifer Torres •

"Buenos días," Pablo says, holding out his hand. "I'm Pab—"

Instead of stopping, Jazmín walks even faster. "Come on." She takes the new girl by the wrist and pulls her toward the third-grade classroom, leaving Pablo and me behind.

Pablo folds his arms. He's wearing his usual crisp, white guayabera and gleaming white sneakers. "That was not very polite," he says, watching Jazmín and the new girl hurry away from us.

I shake my head. "It certainly was not."

Then Pablo sniffs. He wrinkles his nose. "You smell like a tomato."

I huff. "Don't be ridiculous." But when Pablo looks away, I shake out my hair just in case there are any more tomato leaves stuck in there.

We walk together the rest of the way to class.

Ms. Coleman, our new teacher, has placed a small clay flowerpot on each desk. Our names are painted on them, and instead of a plant inside, there are a pair of scissors, a glue stick, and a cactus-shaped bookmark that says *Keep growing!*

Very well-organized! I think.

I find the flowerpot with my name on the desk

behind Pablo's. A*lphabetical order!* I can already tell I'm going to like Ms. Coleman.

As I sit down, I sneak a glance at the new girl's desk in the next row over, right in front of Jazmín's. Her flowerpot says "Esmeralda."

I feel a tap on my shoulder and turn around.

"Have you met the new girl?" Aaron Chu whispers.

"Not exactly," I say. "Have you?"

He shakes his head. "No, but on the way to school this morning, I saw her leaving Jazmín's house."

Pablo spins around. "She was at *Jazmín's* house?"

The bell rings before Aaron can answer. Everyone stops talking. Pablo and I turn to face Ms. Coleman, who is smiling in front of the whiteboard.

"Good morning, third graders," she says. "I hope you're as excited as I am to start this amazing year. I look forward to getting to know each and every one of you. But I want to take a moment to welcome one student in particular. Everyone, meet Esmeralda. She's new to our school this year."

All of us look at the new girl. Her cheeks turn pink, and she twists one of her braids around her finger.

"Esmeralda, we're so glad you're here," Ms. Coleman says. "Would you like to stand and tell us all a little about yourself?"

Esmeralda doesn't answer. She stares down at her lap and keeps twisting her braid.

Some kids start to whisper. Pablo looks over his shoulder at me. *Qué pasa?* he mouths.

I shake my head. I have no idea what's going on. Maybe she's just really nervous?

"Esmeralda?" Ms. Coleman asks again, gently.

Jazmín's hand shoots up. "Ms. Coleman?"

"Yes, Jazmín?"

Jazmín looks around at all of us staring back at her and Esmeralda.

"Esmeralda is my cousin. We call her 'Esme.' She just moved here with her parents—they're staying at my house—and she's pretty shy, that's all."

Ms. Coleman nods. "Thank you, Jazmín. The first day at a brand-new school *can* be a little scary. But I know you'll all help Esme feel right at home."

I think I see Esme's lips twitch up into what might be a tiny smile. But then Jazmín turns and glares straight at Pablo and me.

"That means you two," she growls. "Don't pick on my cousin."

Pablo and I gasp.

• CHAPTER 3 •

Mean Jazmín

Ms. Coleman's eyes widen.

She looks at Pablo, then at me. "I'm sure I can count on both of you to be extra kind to Esme, right?"

"Yes," we mumble. My cheeks burn. I can't believe Jazmín said that in front of everyone! In front of Ms. Coleman! Now Ms. Coleman thinks Pablo and I are *mean*. I am so upset, I could yowl. Exactly like a cat whose tail has been trampled on.

Pablo is angry too. I can tell because his shoulders

are so tense that they're almost touching his ears. I am now determined to make Esme our new best friend. It's the only way to prove Jazmín wrong and show Ms. Coleman she really *can* count on us.

So, later that morning, when I notice that Esme's pencil is a little dull, I lean over and whisper, "It looks like you need a sharper point. You can use one of mine." I try to give her one of my perfectly sharpened pencils, but Jazmín sticks out her hand and blocks me.

"I *said*, leave my cousin alone!" she hisses. "There's nothing wrong with her pencil!"

Then, when we're lining up for recess, Pablo notices that one of the ribbons at the end of Esme's braid has come loose.

"I can fix it for you," he offers. "I happen to be an expert at knots."

It's true. I learned my shoelace technique from Pablo. Not that I'd ever admit it.

But Esme doesn't answer. She bites her lip and looks down.

Jazmín scowls.

"Don't listen to them," she tells Esme, leading her away. "They think they're *so* perfect, but they're not."

Pablo crosses his arms. "That was uncalled for."

"You were only trying to help," I agree.

By lunchtime we are out of ideas. Esme won't talk to us, let alone get to know us.

"It's all because of Jazmín," I grumble, picking the burnt spots off my bean burrito. Mami always thinks I won't notice if the burnt parts are on the inside of the tortilla. But I do.

"More like *Mean* Jazmín," he says. "What did we ever do to her?" He tears another bite off his ham-and-cheese sandwich.

We chew quietly, watching the lunch table where Esme is sitting with Jazmín and her friends. Esme takes a sip from her juice box, then pokes at her cucumber-and-watermelon salad.

"Maybe it's not just us," I observe.

Pablo stops chewing. He swallows. He dabs the corner of his mouth with a napkin. "What do you mean?"

I nod toward Esme. "She isn't talking to *anyone*. Maybe Jazmín was telling the truth, and she's shy. Or maybe . . . she doesn't like it here."

Pablo tilts his head. His eyes glimmer with a new idea.

"Or maybe," he says, "it's something *else*. . . ." His voice trails off mysteriously.

"Something else?"

Pablo uses his napkin to sweep sandwich crumbs off the table and into his empty lunch bag. Once his trash is folded into a neat pile, he drops his head and leans in closer.

"Maybe," he says, his voice low, "Jazmín won't let Esme make any friends. Maybe Esme is trapped. It's just like what happened in this telenovela my mom and I are watching, *Secrets of the Castle*."

I groan. Pablo is a telenovela aficionado, which means he's a huge fan of these dramatic, Spanish-language television shows. The ones Tía Abuela used to act in. He can get a little carried away.

"No, listen," Pablo insists. "It's about a young

duchess who gets sent far from home to live with her aunt to learn how to rule. Except the aunt keeps the duchess locked in the castle and won't let her speak to anyone because the aunt is secretly scheming to take over and become the duchess herself." By the time Pablo finishes, he is nearly out of breath.

I hand him his water bottle. "I'm pretty sure Esme isn't a duchess, Pablo," I say.

Pablo sighs. "I *know* she is not a duchess. But that doesn't mean Jazmín isn't trying to keep her from making friends."

That *might* explain why Jazmín keeps getting in the way every time we try to do something nice for Esme. "But why wouldn't Jazmín want her cousin to have friends?"

Pablo drums his fingers on the table. "We won't know for sure until we investigate."

Suddenly Jazmín stands. For a second I worry

she's overheard us talking about her. My heart races. But then she pulls a stack of envelopes from her backpack. "My mom is throwing a get-to-know-you tardeada for Esme this weekend," she announces.

"A what?" I whisper to Pablo. I'm pretty good at Spanish, but Pablo is better. Maybe from watching all those telenovelas.

"A tar-deh-AH-dah," he repeats slowly. "An afternoon party."

"We hope you can come," Jazmín continues. She starts to pass out invitations, handing one to every third grader in the cafeteria.

But when she gets to the table Pablo and I are sitting at, she walks right by, dropping our invitations back into her bag.

CHAPTER 4

SOMETHING MAGICAL

"Maybe she didn't see us," I suggest. But even I know that's impossible.

"Or maybe," Pablo replies, "she knows we're onto her scheme."

Either way, we have to snag those invitations. We agree that after school each of us will spend thirty minutes thinking up a plan. It will have to wait until after I've had a snack, reorganized my backpack, done my homework, and laid out my clothes for tomorrow, though. I have a schedule to keep, after all.

But when I get home, there's an *unscheduled* delay. "Kitty-Cat, is that you?" Papi calls out as I'm stepping inside. "You're just in time!"

I follow Papi's voice to the living room. His laptop is open on the coffee table, and Carlos is clapping into the camera. *Just in time for this?* One of Carlos's baby videos? Then I hear a cackle that can only belong to one person.

"Tía Abuela!" I shout. I drop my backpack in the middle of the floor—which Coco does all the time, but not me—and race to the computer.

"Catalina, ahí estás!" Tía Abuela smiles back at me on Papi's computer screen.

"Here I am!" I echo. As usual, Tía Abuela is wearing her cat-eye sunglasses with sparkling crystals on the frames. There seems to be a snowstorm behind

her. I lean in closer to the screen. "But where are *you*? Aren't you supposed to be in the Galápagos?"

Tía Abuela laughs. "Por favor! I left Isla Isabela weeks ago. I'm in Chile. Near Cerro Castillo."

The video blurs and wobbles. When Tía Abuela comes back into focus, I notice her earrings. "Are those new?" I ask. "They look like orange blossoms."

Tía Abuela pulls back the hood of her fuzzy parka to give me a better look. "You don't miss a thing, do you, Kitty-Cat?" she asks, and then chuckles.

Nope. I have excellent attention to detail. "They remind me of the orange tree in our backyard," I say.

"Sí, me too," Tía Abuela replies. "That's why I bought them. I was beginning to miss Valle Grande and wanted something that reminded me of home. That's also why I called. Tell me everything! How was the first day of school?"

I want to tell her all about Esme and Mean

Jazmín. Tía Abuela could help me untangle this problem the way she helped me learn to thread a needle and sew my first messy stitches.

I glance over at Papi. He's helping Carlos build a tower with rainbow-colored blocks. You're supposed to put the biggest ones on the bottom of the stack, but their tower is all jumbled and about to topple over.

Even though he looks busy, there's still a chance Papi might be listening, so I don't tell Tía *everything*.

"Well, there's a new girl in our class," I begin. "Her name is Esme. Pablo and I are trying to make friends with her, but it isn't working. I don't think she even *wants* to be our friend."

Tía Abuela presses her lips together and hums. "Pues," she says after a while. "Don't be so quick to think you know how Esme feels. It's like that old saying, 'Caras vemos, corazones no sabemos.'"

She repeats the saying in English to make sure

I understand: "Faces we can see, but hearts we do not know."

It *almost* sounds as if Tía Abuela agrees with Pablo. Like she thinks something else is going on. Something secret.

"Why don't you tell my comadre Josefina about your problem?" Tía Abuela suggests. "You'll see her this afternoon at the Stitch and Share meeting, no?"

I try to make my sigh as quiet as possible, but even thousands of miles away, Tía Abuela can hear it. She pulls her glasses to the bottom of her nose and raises one eyebrow. "You didn't think I'd forget, did you?"

I guess I'm not the only one with excellent attention to detail. After she gave me the sewing pouch and my first lessons, Tía Abuela made me promise to go to the weekly Stitch and Share sessions that her best friend, Josefina, hosts at the Valle Grande

• THE NEW FRIEND FIX •

Central Library. That way, I'd get more practice.

"But the only things Josefina ever lets me sew are pillowcases!" I argue. "I'm ready to move on to something new." I move closer to the computer screen and whisper, "Something *magical*."

Tía Abuela pushes her glasses back up to the bridge of her nose. She waves off my complaint with a flutter of her long, pink fingernails.

"Just go to the meeting, Kitty-Cat," she says finally. "You might learn something—and not just about sewing. You'd better hurry or you're going to be late. And we all know how you feel about being late."

I gulp and check my watch. She's right.

· CHAPTER 5 ·

STITCH AND SHARE

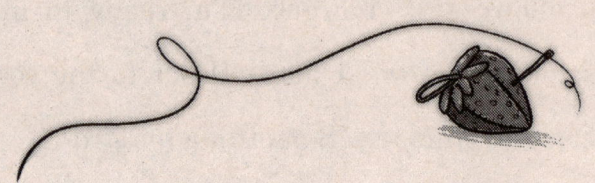

Josefina the Librarian looks up from the dog toy she's stitching when I walk into the Valle Grande Central Library community room. I am huffing and puffing after sprinting all the way down the hill from my house to get here.

It is exactly two minutes before the Stitch and Share meeting is scheduled to start. In other words, I am right on time.

"Prompt as usual, Catalina," Josefina says. She

sets down her sewing project and stands to greet me.

"What do you think about working on a *pillowcase* today?" Her eyes sparkle when she says "pillowcase." As if it's the most exciting project ever. As if I haven't already sewn four of them.

The metal folding chairs in the community room are arranged in a circle. At the center is a big plastic bin filled with scraps of fabric donated by library visitors. Josefina opens the bin and begins rummaging through the cloth. She digs through flower prints, polka dots, stripes.

I take a step toward her. "I do love pillowcases," I say, peering into the bin. "But now I think I'm ready for something different. Something a little more . . . challenging."

And interesting, I want to add. But I don't. What I'd really like to sew is a new disfraz. If I could disguise myself as a magician or a party princess, I might be able to sneak into Esme's tardeada even without an invitation.

But I know Josefina the Librarian would never let me work on something *that* interesting.

"Here it is!" Josefina announces as if she hasn't heard me at all. "As soon as I saw it, I knew it would be perfect for you. Or should I say 'purrrfect'?"

Josefina holds up a piece of fabric. It's pale blue and covered with kittens.

Of course.

Kittens playing with yarn balls. Kittens curled on blankets. Kittens with flowers behind their furry ears.

I want to tell her I'm getting too old for all this kitten stuff. But, the truth is, the fabric *is* kind of cute.

"It will make the *purrrfect* pillowcase," I admit. I take the fabric and choose a seat.

Josefina claps. "I knew you'd love it. The pattern reminds me of a calico kitten I used to foster. We called her 'Guapa' because she was so pretty. She used to love playing with yarn and ribbons."

It sounds like Josefina misses Guapa. I unfold the fabric and smooth it over my lap. "I could give you the pillowcase when I'm finished," I offer. "To remind you of Guapa."

Then I lower my voice and mutter, "I can *always* make another one."

Josefina pats my shoulder. "That would be delightful, Catalina. Gracias."

More people arrive at the Stitch and Share session. Josefina calls us sewists. I like the word because it sounds kind of like "artist." Everyone brings their latest project and shares what they're working on. If anyone runs into trouble, there are plenty of people to give advice. I get *lots* of advice.

Mrs. Glass, who always works on quilts, sits down next to me with her big wooden hoop. This time there is a patchwork of green and yellow squares stretched inside it.

"Who is it for?" I ask.

Mrs. Glass smiles as she takes the rest of her supplies out of her sewing bag. "It's for my nephew's family," she answers. "They're expecting a new baby."

Anthony Becerra sits down a few chairs over. Of all the sewists, he's the "closest" to my age—and he's in high school. Anthony is making dog and cat toys for the animal shelter as part of a community service project. Josefina and some of the other sewists have volunteered to help.

As everyone settles in, I open up my sewing kit—not the magic one, just an old cookie tin with needles and thread and other supplies inside. Tía Abuela gave it to me for practice. I choose a spool of thread that matches the blue kitten fabric, snip some off, and thread my needle.

When I first started sewing, it took me five or six tries to get the thread to slip through that teensy eye. Sometimes more. Now I do it on my first attempt.

Josefina notices. "Soon you'll be sewing quilts, just like Mrs. Glass," she says.

I'd settle for chew toys.

Josefina must be able to read my thoughts. Or maybe she can just read my face, because the next thing she says is, "I know you want to move faster, but your Tía Abuela told me it was very important that you learn to make your stitches nice and strong. And practice is the best way to make progress."

Ms. Yoo chuckles to herself.

"I was remembering the night I rushed through

sewing the buttons on a new dress so that I could make it to a party on time," she says. "Half of them fell off. I had to hold the dress together with staples!"

I feel my cheeks turn red, thinking about how embarrassing that must've been. I'd be in big trouble if a magical disfraz ever fell apart while I was wearing it.

"You think that's bad?" Mr. Hart pauses in the middle of a stitch. "You should hear about the time I decided to shorten my uniform pants. I didn't double-check the measurements, and one leg turned out longer than the other! I had to deliver the mail like that all day!"

I would have triple-checked the measurements. Still, I squint down at my stitches. Maybe a little more practice isn't such a bad idea. And while I sew, I can think up a way to make Esme see what a great friend I am.

· CHAPTER 6 ·

Incognito

The next afternoon Pablo and I creep behind a tree. We stare at Jazmín's backpack as she and Esme start walking home from school.

"Do you think our invitations are still in there?" he asks.

I nod. "I saw them when Jazmín took out her pencil case this morning."

Pablo unzips the front pocket of his backpack. He takes out two mango-flavored lollipops. He lowers his voice. "Here's what we're going to do. You run up and offer these to Jazmín and Esme. They probably won't take them. Jazmín might even yell at you to go away. While she's distracted, I'll sneak up behind her, open her backpack, and grab the invitations. It'll be just like a scene from *Diary of a Thief*!"

It's not that I don't like Pablo's plan. It's just that I have a better one. I came up with it during Stitch and Share. Only, I can't tell him about it because it involves my sweatshirt. *That* sweatshirt.

"Sorry, Pablo, but there's . . . something I need to do first," I reply. "Don't worry, though. We'll get those invitations."

"Don't *worry*?" he says. "The tardeada is this weekend. We don't have much time."

What can I say to convince him?

"I've already put the tardeada on my schedule," I say. "And if it's on my schedule—"

"You'll be there." Pablo finishes my sentence for me. "I hope you're right." He tucks the lollipops into his pocket and starts walking home.

Not until Pablo has turned the corner do I dare

to dig the kitten sweatshirt out of my backpack. I slip my arms inside, zip it up, and then put on the hood. Once again, I am incognito.

Disguised, I make my way to Jazmín's house.

When I get there, I find her and Esme outside, doing their homework on the front porch.

I duck behind a hedge in the Galindos' front yard and listen.

"What if no one comes?" Esme asks.

They're talking about the party! I poke my head out to hear better.

"Of course they'll come," Jazmín said. "I told you. I only invited the nice people."

Only invited the nice *people?*

I leap out from behind the hedge. "Hey! What's that supposed to mean?"

Except I'm still disguised as a cat, so it comes out like a snarl and a hiss.

Whoops.

Esme and Jazmín look up at the same time. I should probably run away while I still can. But I still need those invitations.

Esme points. "A cat!"

Jazmín frowns. "Shoo, go away. Mom doesn't like

cats in her plants." Typical. I'm starting to think Pablo is right. Jazmín *is* mean.

Esme stops writing and slowly walks down the front steps.

"Wait!" she says. "This cat looks familiar."

I do?

"She *does?*" Jazmín says.

Esme kneels on the grass, still giving me a lot of space. "Mm-hmm. She looks a lot like my neighbor's cat, León. León was a bit scruffy too."

"A bit *scruffy?*" I yowl. Even as a cat, I'm sure I am perfectly put together. I whisk some hair off my face.

"Look, she's cleaning herself!" Esme squeals, inching forward. "Isn't she so cute?"

Jazmín's frown softens. "She reminds you of your neighbor's cat? At your old house?" she asks. "Maybe we can get her to come closer."

Jazmín goes into the house and comes back with a can of tuna.

"Here, kitty," Jazmín says, waving the can at me.

I don't really like tuna. But this is my best chance to get close enough to Jazmín's backpack to snatch the invitations. I trot along the stone walkway, past Esme, up the steps, and onto the porch.

From here I can see what Esme has been working on. It's our spelling list. But instead of writing the words out five times each like Ms. Coleman told us to, Esme has been drawing a picture. It's a house with a red tile roof and a garden bursting with pink and orange roses.

Jazmín waves the can again. "Come on, kitty-cat, just a little closer."

I take another step. Then Jazmín says quietly, "As soon as I give her the tuna, you grab her and take her inside. Maybe my mom will let you keep her. To remind you of home."

Oh no! I whip my head around just as Esme is lunging for me, arms outstretched.

I leap out of the way. Esme screams as I scramble over the drawing, scattering her crayons.

Before I can catch my balance, Jazmín tries to grab me. I manage to duck under her arms, but not without knocking over her backpack. Everything spills out—pencils, pens, library books, and the two party invitations that were supposed to have gone to Pablo and me.

I dash down the steps right as Señora Galindo steps to the door. "What's going on out here?"

Then, as I race back out to the sidewalk, I hear her add, "Jazmín, I thought you said you handed out *all* the invitations."

• CHAPTER 7 •

Messy Business

That evening Papi takes his brown-bag dinner from the refrigerator, kisses Coco, Carlos, and me on our foreheads, and then leaves for the community college where he teaches a math class three nights a week.

"Adiós!" he says, and waves. "I'll see you all in the morning."

Coco and I set the table while Mami stirs a pot of fideo noodles on the stove. Carlos sits on the kitchen floor, jangling Mami's car keys.

"What's wrong with you?" Coco asks. "You've been in a bad mood ever since I got home."

I turn my head so Coco can't see my face. "Nothing."

Nothing except that I didn't get those invitations. And now they might not even be in Jazmín's backpack anymore.

But I don't feel like explaining everything to Coco, so I try to change the subject. "Shouldn't you be out skateboarding with your friends?"

Coco pulls her baseball cap so low on her forehead that I can't see her eyes anymore.

"Not in the mood," she says. "First I forgot my locker combination. Then I brought the wrong books to science class. And *then* I got lost on the way to history. *Again.* I wish I were back at Valle Grande Elementary, where I knew how everything worked."

It's strange to hear Coco sound nervous. She usually loves a new adventure. It takes me a long time to decide what to say.

"Well, it was only the second day," I tell her. "I bet it'll be exactly like learning a new skateboarding trick. At first you'll mess up a lot. But pretty soon it'll be like you were doing it forever."

Coco nudges me in the ribs. "I just hope I don't mess up as much as you do when you're learning a trick."

She is already starting to feel better. I can tell.

Coco lifts Carlos into his high chair, and I clear some space in the middle of the table for Mami to set down the soup pot. As soon as she does, her phone rings.

"You girls start feeding your brother," she says. "I'll be right back."

Both of us look at the soup spoon, but neither of

us reaches for it. Feeding Carlos is messy business. Especially when it comes to noodles.

"I think it's *your* turn," Coco says, spooning some fideo into his bowl before passing it to me.

"But he likes it better when *you* feed him," I insist, passing the bowl back.

Carlos screeches. In the hallway Mami covers the phone with her hand and shoots us a warning look.

"Niñas! Por favor!"

"We'll take turns," Coco offers. "You go first."

"Fine." I scoop some fideo into Carlos's mouth and try to move my hand away before half-chewed pieces of noodle and tomato land on it.

Mami holds the phone to her ear again. "I'm sorry, Rosa. What were you saying about a stray cat?"

Rosa? That's Jazmín's mom. I feed Carlos another bite of fideo and strain to listen.

"You know, we have been having some trouble with a stray cat too," Mami is saying. She pauses. "Sí! Gray with a diamond-shaped patch of white fur on her forehead. I wonder if it's the same cat!"

I drop Carlos's spoon, and it clatters onto his high-chair tray. I pick it up, wipe it off, and hand it to Coco. "Your turn."

Then I nod toward Mami and hold a finger up to my lips. Coco nods back. She'll keep quiet.

I tiptoe into the living room and toward the hallway to hear better.

"What a lovely way to make some friends," Mami says. "Oh, I see. . . . Ah. . . . Mm-hmm."

It is impossible to know what's going on when I can't hear Señora Galindo.

"Of course," Mami says. "You too. Goodbye!"

She clicks off the phone, and I bolt back to my chair. Mami gets to the table moments later, and I pretend I haven't been eavesdropping. "Who was that?" I ask.

Coco snorts.

Mami ignores her. "That was Señora Galindo. She's hosting a tardeada on Saturday so Jazmín's cousin Esme can get to know her classmates."

I scoot to the edge of my chair. I wait for Mami to say I'm invited.

But she doesn't.

She serves herself some fideo. She chews and swallows.

"Oh!" she says.

"Yes?" I answer, sitting up straighter. Here it comes. I bet she'll tell me now.

"I just had an idea," Mami continues. "What if I make Esme's parents a batch of my famous salsa verde?"

I slouch. Wrong again.

"I don't know," Coco teases. "We want to welcome them, not scare them away."

"Coco!" Mami presses her hand over her heart, pretending she's offended.

I actually *am* offended. "Why should we bring them anything if I wasn't even invited to the party?"

Mami winks. "Didn't you hear?" she asks. "Because I thought for sure I noticed someone listening near the hallway. Well. It turns out your invitation got misplaced by mistake. Jazmín will bring it to school tomorrow."

Looks like I managed to snag those invitations after all!

· CHAPTER 8 ·

Too Much

I can't wait to tell Pablo the good news. But when I spot him standing outside our classroom the next morning, I can see he already knows.

"Como el gato que se comió la manteca," I say as I walk up to him.

Pablo scrunches his nose. "Like the cat that ate the butter?" he asks. "What is that supposed to mean?" Then he sucks in a nervous breath and looks down at his shirt. "I didn't spill any butter on myself, did I?"

I laugh. "No, it's a saying Tía Abuela taught me. It means 'You look like you're very pleased with yourself.'"

Pablo grins. "As a matter of fact, I am." He opens his backpack and takes out his binder. Pablo has special dividers with tabs *and* pockets. I tried to convince Mami and Papi to buy me a set, but they said the last thing I need is more organizational supplies. If they could see how orderly Pablo's notebook is, I'm sure they'd change her minds.

Pablo flips to a tab near the back. He reaches into the pocket, pulls out an envelope, and hands it to me. "Open it."

"Let me guess," I say. "Is it an invitation to Esme's get-to-know-you tardeada?"

Pablo snatches the envelope back. "How'd you

know? Jazmín only gave it to me this morning."

I explain how Señora Galindo called Mami last night and how I'm getting an invitation too. "She says our invitations got misplaced by mistake."

We both know it was *not* a mistake.

"At least we get to go," he says. "Now all I need to do is find Esme the perfect welcome-to-the-neighborhood gift. Then she'll know Jazmín was wrong about me." He flips to another section of his notebook. "I've narrowed it down to five ideas."

I try to peek at Pablo's list, but he slams the notebook shut.

"Don't worry, I already have my *own* list," I fib. "And Esme's going to love *my* gift best."

I turn and march into the classroom.

Pablo follows close behind. "How can you be so sure you know what she likes? You've barely talked to her."

"Well, neither have you," I say as I take my seat.

Luckily, Ms. Coleman gives us a chance to fix that. Later that morning, when it's time for social studies, she divides the class into small groups. "Esme, why don't you join Catalina and Pablo?" she says.

We slide our desks over to make room, but Esme doesn't move. She looks down at the floor and twists one of her braids.

Jazmín raises her hand. "Ms. Coleman," she says before she's even called on. "Shouldn't Esme be in my group? Since she's my cousin?"

Pablo looks at me, eyes wide. "See? *Just* like *Secrets of the Castle*," he murmurs.

Ms. Coleman stands beside Jazmín's desk. "It's very thoughtful of you to look out for your cousin. But it will be good for Esme to make other friends too. And Catalina and Pablo will take good care of her." She turns to us. "Won't you?"

We nod eagerly. Finally Esme moves her desk toward ours.

Once everyone is in a group, Ms. Coleman gives the instructions. "First I want you to list the communities you belong to," she says. "As many as you can think of. Then, in your groups, talk about which communities you and your partners have in common."

I can't tell if Esme is listening. She's doodling at the edges of her notebook paper. It's the same house I saw in the drawing on the Galindos' porch, with pink and orange roses in the front. This time there's a gray cat next to it.

"All right, everyone," Ms. Coleman says. "Go ahead and get started, and let me know if you need any help."

Normally Pablo and I follow directions as carefully as we can. But this might be our only chance to get to know Esme before the tardeada, so we take it.

"I see you like to draw," Pablo says. "What kind of pencils are your favorite? Colored pencils? Mechanical pencils? Grease pencils?"

Esme hesitates. "I don't know," she mumbles without taking her eyes off her paper. "Just . . . regular pencils, I guess?"

Pablo scribbles something in his notebook.

"What about erasers?" I ask. Erasers are very important. They help you fix mistakes.

"Um . . . aren't they all sort of . . . the same?"

• THE NEW FRIEND FIX •

Esme says. Her voice is so quiet, I can hardly hear her.

Pablo smacks his hands against the desk. "All the same? But there's pink erasers and gum erasers and erasers you can roll up like clay—"

I interrupt him. Pablo can talk about erasers for hours. "What is that, anyway?" I ask, tapping the corner of Esme's paper. "Why do you keep drawing that house?"

Esme looks up. Her cheeks are

bright pink, and her eyes are shiny with tears.

"I don't know," she says. "I just like drawing it!" Then she gets up and runs toward the door.

The whole class goes silent. Everyone stares at Pablo and me. Jazmín jumps up from her seat and glares at us.

"I knew this was going to happen!" she shouts. "You're just too mean and too . . . *much*!"

• CHAPTER 9 •

What Really Happened

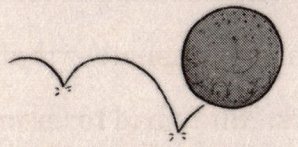

Ms. Coleman asks Pablo and me to stay in from recess. She calls us to her desk and folds her hands on top of it. I hold my breath.

"I know you didn't mean to hurt Esme's feelings," she tells us.

I let my air out, so relieved that my knees wobble. "We really didn't," I say.

"We were just trying to get to know her," Pablo

adds. "I don't know why she got so upset. I think it's Jazmín. She's—"

Ms. Coleman holds up a hand to stop us.

"I believe you. Just remember that Esme is new," Ms. Coleman says. "She's had to leave her home and her friends. And I think she might be a little sensitive. Give her some time to come out of her shell."

I'm glad Ms. Coleman believes us. Unfortunately, no one on the playground does.

"What did you say to Esme?" Aaron asks. "I know you two can be picky, but I thought you'd leave the new kid alone."

"We were *not* being picky," I protest. "We were only trying to plan the perfect present!" But Aaron isn't really listening.

Pablo and I walk over to the four-square courts. I love four square because there are rules that tell you what's allowed and what's not. But when we line up at the court, Gracie Davis grabs the ball and holds it under her arm. "Are you here to tell us we're doing it wrong? Just like you told Esme?"

"That is *not* what happened!" I say.

"According to Jazmín, it is," Bruno Zamora replies. "She said that you two were picking on Esme and her drawing and you made her cry."

This is so unfair. "Let's go, Pablo," I say. "We need to find Jazmín."

"You're right," he says. "This is all *her* fault. We need to figure out what she's up to before it gets worse. We have to warn Esme."

I'm pretty sure Pablo is wrong about Jazmín. After what I saw yesterday, I think she might be trying to protect Esme. We just need to explain that she doesn't have to protect her from *us*.

We find them on the climbing dome. I haven't played on it since first grade, when I hung upside down and my shirt slipped, and everyone saw my belly button.

Jazmín and Esme are sitting at the very top. I cup my hands around my mouth and call up to them.

"Can we talk to you?"

Jazmín turns to Esme. "Don't worry, I'll handle this." She scowls down at us. "What do you two want? Haven't you caused enough trouble?"

"Please?" I say. "We just want to explain what *really* happened in class earlier."

Jazmín jumps down from the climbing dome and lands in front of us.

"You don't have to explain anything," she says. "I already know what happened. You were picking on Esme's work the way you always do. It's just like in second grade, when you told me my dinosaur diorama was all wrong. I worked really hard on that!"

The dinosaur diorama? That was a whole year ago. And Pablo and I were only trying to help. I thought everyone wanted their project to be perfect.

"You had a stegosaurus and a tyrannosaurus together in your shoebox!" Pablo cries. "They lived in completely different periods. We thought you would want to know so you could fix it."

I would have wanted to know.

Jazmín turns her head away from us. "Well, it made me feel really bad. And I don't want you to make Esme feel bad too. I only gave you an invitation because Mom said I had to. But you are *not* welcome."

CHAPTER 10

A New Plan

I am so angry with Jazmín. For calling us mean. For refusing to listen when we tried to explain ourselves.

I'm even a little mad at Esme, too. I know she's new, but she could have said something. She knows Pablo and I weren't picking on her.

Doesn't she?

I try to imagine what Tía Abuela would do. She

wouldn't give up, that's for sure. She would think of a new plan.

It's amazing how many problems you can solve with a needle and thread, Tía Abuela once told me. And I start to wonder if sewing can fix this situation.

I've got it, I decide as I march home from school. *I'll use the magic sewing kit to create a hornet disfraz to wear to Esme's party.* No one will be able to enjoy the tardeada with me buzzing around. The party will be completely ruined.

But by the next morning, I don't really feel like scheming anymore. Jazmín should have given Pablo and me a chance to tell our side of the story. But maybe *we* should have stopped to think about how all our attention to detail makes others feel. Especially someone who doesn't know us very well. Like Esme.

In the kitchen, Mami is packing lunches for Coco

and me while Papi is feeding Carlos his oatmeal. Somehow it is even messier than the fideo.

"Have you thought about what you might like to give Esme as a welcome gift?" Mami asks. "The tardeada is coming up soon. I'm surprised you haven't already given me a list. You're usually so organized."

I sit down next to Coco and serve myself some oatmeal. "Actually, I don't think I want to go anymore." I try to make my voice sound breezy. Like it's no big deal.

It doesn't work. Mami freezes with one hand on the open refrigerator door. Papi puts down the spoonful of oatmeal he was about to feed Carlos. Coco's mouth hangs open, even though it is full of toast.

"But you were so mad when you thought you weren't invited," Coco says.

"I wasn't *that* mad," I say, stirring my oatmeal because I don't want to look at their faces. "And anyway, I need to color-coordinate my closet on Saturday. All my clothes are out of order."

Mami frowns. "But you can do that any weekend."

Coco rolls her eyes. "She does that *every* weekend."

I stick my tongue out at her. "At least I wear fresh clothes every day. Unlike *you*."

She is still wearing that smelly old flannel.

"I told you," Coco says. "It's lucky."

Mami takes a banana from the bowl on the counter and zips up her purse. "Pues, we won't make you go to the party," she says. "But I'm disappointed that you want to miss this chance to welcome Esme to the neighborhood."

Papi nods. "Especially since you were so looking forward to meeting her."

What a mess. Not only has Jazmín turned the class against me, but now Mami and Papi are disappointed too. I want to tell them what happened, but they'll probably just say I've been too quisquillosa. It's a fun word to say: kee-skee-YO-sah. But it's not so fun once you know what it means. "Persnickety." In other words, "picky."

"I'll think about it," I promise.

Papi smiles and feeds Carlos another bite of oatmeal.

Mami walks over and gives my shoulders a squeeze. "Bueno," she says. "That's all I ask."

I'm not very hungry, so after two more swallows of oatmeal, I put on my backpack. "I'm leaving for school," I say.

"Hold up!" Coco answers. "I'll come with you as far as the corner."

This time I wait for her.

When we get outside, Coco drops her skateboard onto the sidewalk and hops on. She pushes slowly alongside me until we are halfway down the block.

"So what's the real reason you don't want to go to the party?" she asks. "Is Esme weird or something? Is she *mean*?"

I can't hold it in anymore. "No!" I burst out. "But she thinks *I* am. And now everyone else does too." I explain what happened, how Pablo and I were only trying to be friendly, but everything went wrong.

We reach the corner. Coco slows her skateboard to a stop, flicks it up, and catches it under her arm. I notice a Valle Grande Elementary School sticker on the bottom of the board.

"Shouldn't you have a middle school sticker now?" I ask.

Coco rubs the sticker with her thumb. "I don't know," she says. "It makes me feel better having the elementary school sticker with me. Kind of like my flannel."

The crosswalk signal lights up. It's time for Coco

to go in one direction and me to go in the other.

"Listen," Coco says before she jumps back onto her board. "It sounds like Esme and Jazmín can't tell that you were only trying to be friendly. Maybe you can find a way to *show* them."

• CHAPTER 11 •

Surprise Sewing

Coco's advice reminds me of what Tía Abuela told me earlier in the week. How you can see what's on someone's face, but not always what's in their heart.

Pablo thought Jazmín was being rude to us—and she kind of *was*. But it wasn't part of an evil plot. In her heart, she was trying to look out for her cousin.

Just like how Esme and Jazmín might think Pablo and I are being persnickety. But, really, we're just trying to be friends.

By the end of the school day, I think I've figured out a way to show them. I ask Pablo to meet me at the library.

"This is a pleasant surprise," Josefina the Librarian says when we get there. "But since I wasn't expecting you, I'm afraid I've already shelved most of the books."

Putting books back precisely where they belong is one of our favorite things to do at the library. Josefina usually saves them for us.

"That's okay," I say. "That's not why we're here."

"It's not?" Pablo and Josefina say together.

"I thought you were trying to cheer me up," Pablo says, shaking his head. "It was working."

"Don't worry," I tell him. "This is even better. Señora Josefina, I know we don't have a Stitch and Share meeting today, but can Pablo and I use some fabric from the scrap bin? I have an idea."

Josefina looks around the library. Ernest, her assistant, is leading a coding class. Some high schoolers are finishing their homework. In the lobby, a visitor is admiring a shimmering green gown that used to belong to Tía Abuela. She donated it to the library over the summer, and it reminds me that strong stitches aren't just for fashion. They're also for fixing. Maybe they can even fix friendships.

"It sure looks like a good time for a surprise sewing session to me!" Josefina says.

When she gets back with the bin, I reach in and pull out two pieces of flowered fabric I noticed during Stitch and Share.

"There's a new girl at school, and we want to welcome her," I explain. "She keeps drawing a picture of a house with lots of flowers in the front. I think it must be where she used to live, and I bet she misses it. If I make her a pillowcase with this flowery fabric, maybe it will remind her of home. The way the kitten pillowcase reminded you of Guapa." And the way Coco's sticker reminds her of Valle Grande Elementary.

Josefina doesn't say anything for a few long moments. I watch the second hand on her cat-shaped watch tick by. I worry that she won't let us use the fabric after all. Or that she thinks it's a terrible idea.

But then she claps her hands together. "Fantástico! It's a good thing you've sewn so many pillowcases. You're practically an expert now."

I *am*. And this pillowcase is going to be my best yet. I sit down with the fabric at one of the study tables and take the cookie-tin sewing kit out of my backpack. "Vamos! Let's get started! Sit down, Pablo. I'll teach you."

Pablo does not sit down.

"Aren't you forgetting something?" he asks. "What about Jazmín? She won't let us near her cousin."

He has a point.

"Well . . . ," I begin. "We . . . could . . . make a present for Jazmín too! Maybe that will change her mind."

As soon as I've said it aloud, I know it's a perfect plan. I hop to my feet and rummage through the scrap bin. Josefina really needs to organize all this fabric.

"A *dinosaur* pillowcase," I say.

Josefina clears her throat. "You can make as many pillowcases as you like," she says. "But I'm afraid you won't find any dinosaur fabric in there."

Pablo reaches into the bin. "No problem!" he says. "There's lots of plain fabric. I can *draw* some dinosaurs on it."

"You know," Josefina says, "I think I even have some fabric markers left over from one of our craft workshops."

While Josefina goes to look for the markers, Pablo heads into the Prehistoric Life section of the library to look for books about dinosaurs.

"I want them to be perfect," he says.

"Just make sure you draw a stegosaurus *and* a tyrannosaurus," I say. Then I smooth out my fabric and start measuring.

· CHAPTER 12 ·

Right on Time

When she finds out what I'm up to, Mami lets me stay up an hour past my bedtime to work on the pillowcases. It still takes me until Friday night to finish.

Before wrapping them up, I admire the stitches. Nice and strong. I wish Tía Abuela were here to see them. I know she'd be proud, and not just of my sewing.

On Saturday, the day of the tardeada, Pablo

meets me on the sidewalk outside Jazmín and Esme's house, exactly as we planned.

His hands are jammed into his pockets. His eyes dart nervously left and right.

"Right on time," he says when he sees me.

In other words, we are early. The party won't start for another thirty minutes.

"Of course I am," I say. Together we walk toward the house. The back gate is open, and a sign on it says BIENVENIDOS! COME RIGHT IN!

Already the sound of party music and the smell of carne asada cooking on a grill spill over the yard.

Pablo pauses. "Are you sure about this?" he asks. "What if Jazmín is mad that we came? What if she wants us to leave?"

That would be even worse than what happened at school. For a second I hesitate too. I wish I had come incognito.

But then Esme and Jazmín wouldn't be able to see what's on my face *or* in my heart.

"We don't have to stay if they don't want us to," I tell Pablo. "We'll just give them our gifts and leave. That's what we really came for, after all."

We each take a deep breath and step through the gate.

In the backyard Jazmín is spreading out a tablecloth, and Esme is hanging a papel picado banner. Jazmín stops to help Esme tie off one end, but then she notices us and lets it flutter to the ground.

"I didn't expect to see *you* here," Jazmín says.

Señora Galindo walks out the back door carrying a bowl full of tortilla chips in one arm and a vase of flowers in the other. She arranges them on one of the tables.

"Don't be silly." She turns to Pablo and me. "Of course we expected you. Maybe not this early, but you're just in time to help Jazmín and Esmeralda with the decorations. I'm going to start mixing the punch."

Señora Galindo goes back inside. Jazmín tosses a bag of balloons at me. "I guess you can blow these up while Esme and I finish hanging the banner."

Pablo and I set the gift bags down. We each pull a balloon from the plastic bag and start blowing. Esme and Jazmín take the papel picado to the other end of the patio.

"This isn't working," Pablo whispers.

I let go of my balloon. It whirs to the ground with a sad whoosh.

That's how I feel. Like all the air has sputtered out of my great idea.

It looks like I'm going to have to be bold. Like Tía Abuela. (Although, I can't help but think it would be easier with a pair of cat-eye sunglasses.)

I pick up the gift bags and walk over to Jazmín and Esme.

"We won't stay if you don't want us to," I say. "We're only here to drop off these presents. We made them ourselves." I hold out the gift bags. Jazmín and Esme exchange cautious glances before taking them.

Esme opens hers first. Carefully she removes the tissue paper and pulls out the pillowcase. She runs her fingers over the pink flowers on the front, then

flips it over to look at the red flowers on the back. I have to slap my hand over my mouth to stop myself from asking if she likes it. It feels like forever until she says anything.

"My house—the house we used to live in—had a big garden in front with pink and orange roses," Esme says finally. "This reminds me of them. How did you know?"

"I saw you drawing those flowers, and I guessed it was your old house," I say. "I didn't mean to hurt your feelings."

"I thought you were teasing me about my drawing," Esme says. "I guess I was wrong."

Now I twist some of *my* hair. "Well, we did get a little overexcited, and we probably should have given you some space since Jazmín did tell everyone you were shy," I admit. "Sorry about that."

Esme smiles.

"Aren't you going to open yours?" Pablo asks Jazmín.

She takes the pillowcase out of the gift bag and shakes it out. I'm really proud of this one. After Pablo drew the dinosaurs, I stitched on eyes and scales with some help from Josefina.

"Now I understand why you thought we were picking on your diorama," Pablo says, "but, I promise, we were only trying to be helpful. And you were right all along! A stegosaurus and tyrannosaurus *do* look pretty good together."

"Maybe," Jazmín says slowly, "I should have given you a chance to explain."

I spring up onto the tips of my toes. "Does this mean we can stay for the party?"

Esme rocks from her left foot to her right. "You can stay . . . *if*—"

"If?" Pablo and I say at the same time.

Esme giggles. "*If* you help us with this banner. It's all crooked!"

Pablo and I look at each other and grin. We are *just* the people for the job.

"Don't worry," Pablo exclaims, grabbing one end. "We'll make sure it's absolutely perfect!"

"We're going to need a ruler!" I shout, taking hold of the other end.

"And a level!" Pablo adds. "A laser one if you have it."

Esme shuffles backward and reaches for her braid again. Jazmín's hand moves to her hip.

Too much?

"Or . . . maybe," I say, "we'll just do the best we can without any special measuring tools."

Jazmín smiles. "That," she agrees, "sounds like a great plan."

· The New Friend Fix ·

And even though the banner is a little crooked when the other guests begin to arrive, it is still *perfectly* fine.

Turn the page for a sneak peek at Catalina's next magical adventure!

· CHAPTER 1 ·

*F*LUTTER

It's after school on Monday, and the auditorium is filled with students practicing for the Valle Grande Elementary talent show. Auditions are at the end of this week.

I creep past a group of fourth graders, tap-dancing side by side next to a second grader performing a tae kwon do demonstration.

Behind them, Aaron Chu, a third grader in my class, rehearses his magic act. He swooshes his cape.

He waves his hands over a black top hat. He taps the edge of the hat with his wand. I watch, waiting to see what will happen.

When nothing does, Aaron peers into the hat and shrugs.

I shudder. I'd hate for my act to go wrong. That's why I'm sneaking through the auditorium. Somewhere in this room is the formula for a perfect performance, and I'm going to find it. I need to make sure my group has an amazing audition and gets picked for the show.

The best part is, none of the other kids notice me. Not really. When they look in my direction, all they see is a yellow-winged butterfly. That's because last summer my tía abuela—her name is Catalina Castañeda too—gave me a special sewing kit.

It might not *look* very special, just an old, worn-out velvet pouch. But the needle and thread inside have the power to sew magical disguises.

Over the weekend, I sewed butterfly wings onto one of my old sweaters. (It was missing a button anyway. I could have sewn on a new one, but it wouldn't have matched the others, and I can't stand it when things don't match). Then I added antennae to one of my hairbands. The perfect disfraz! Now anyone who sees me thinks I'm a butterfly. I am *incognito*.

Tía Abuela told me to save the magic for times when I *really* need it. Once my spool of silvery magical thread is gone, it's gone for good.

This is one of those times when I need my magic. After all, my bandmates and I will be performing a song that Tía Abuela made famous back when she was still a telenovela actress. We can't make any mistakes.

I flutter behind Esme Galindo and her cousin

Jazmín. They wear swirling blue skirts as they practice a folklórico dance.

Suddenly Jazmín stops in the middle of a step.

"What happened?" Esme asks. "Did you forget what comes next?"

They definitely need more practice.

Jazmín shakes her head. "No, but I thought I saw Catalina."

Uh-oh. Maybe my disfraz isn't working. I duck behind a cardboard tree some fifth graders are using as a prop in their skit.

"Shouldn't she be with her own group?" Esme asks.

"You know Catalina," Jazmín continues. "She probably wanted to give us some of her helpful hints."

Esme giggles, and they start dancing again.

I *might* have a reputation for being a bit of a perfectionist. *Who doesn't want to be perfect?* I almost wonder aloud. Instead I look over my shoulder to make sure the butterfly wings are still attached.

Tía Abuela warned me that the magic would only be as strong as my stitches. And these are coming loose! I need to get out of this disfraz before anyone else notices!

While the fifth graders argue over their lines, I yank off the wings and slip out of the sweater. I tuck everything under my arm, then step out from behind the carboard tree and find my group at the other side of the auditorium.

We call ourselves Banda La Chispa in honor of Tía Abuela. Her fans know her as La Chispa, "the spark," because she was always so bright and dazzling onscreen.

Ruthie Rosario sits behind her drum set. Soledad Beltrán has her guitar strapped over her shoulder. Pablo Blanco, my best friend—and biggest rival—stands next to his keyboard, tapping his foot. He scowls when he sees me. "You're late," he says.

Impossible. No one cares about punctuality as much as I do. Except for Pablo, that is. I look down at my watch and frown. Unfortunately, he's right.

"Only thirty-six seconds," I say.

"Thirty-seven," Pablo argues. "And anyway, late is late. Where were you?"

I hesitate. So far I haven't revealed the secret of the magic sewing kit to anyone.

Luckily, Ruthie interrupts before I have to answer.

"Cool hairband!" she says. "Animal accessories are my favorite!"

I feel the top of my head. I'm still wearing the butterfly antennae. "Um, thanks," I mumble, my cheeks turning warm. Pablo snorts. Normally I am perfectly put together.

Soledad hands me the tambourine we borrowed from the music room. "Now that we're all here," she says, "let's run through the song from the very beginning."

Ruthie taps out the rhythm with her drumsticks. "Uno, dos, tres, cuatro!" Soledad counts. She begins to strum, then nods at Pablo, who presses down on the keys. I start shaking the tambourine. When we get to the chorus, I open my mouth to sing. Only, I can hardly keep up with Ruthie's beat.

Pablo's notes clash with Soledad's chords, and we all sound a little . . . off-key.

When the song ends, I cringe. Part of me wants to run back to that cardboard tree to hide again. Maybe we can still back out of the auditions. Then I remind myself of something Tía Abuela taught me when I was first learning to sew: progress takes practice. *And* patience. Sometimes a *lot* of patience.

"Don't worry," I reassure everyone. "We still have a few more days to get better."

"Are you kidding?" Soledad shouts. "That was amazing! And so much fun! We are obviously going to make the talent show."

But I'm not so sure.

· CHAPTER 2 ·

Special Delivery

I can't open the door at first when I get home from school. Something is blocking it. My older sister, Coco, probably dumped her enormous backpack in the entryway. *Again.* This is exactly why I asked Mami to install those special hooks on our bedroom wall. I thought that if the backpacks had a special place to hang, maybe Coco would stop leaving hers on the floor. It doesn't seem to be working.

"Co—" I start to complain as I shove the door

open. Then I look down. It isn't Coco's backpack that's blocking the way. It's a big box. Addressed to me! The postage on top says it came from Colombia.

And the handwriting tells me who sent it: Tía Abuela.

Ever since she retired from acting, Tía Abuela spends most of her time traveling the world. Wherever she goes, she finds a way to send packages home to Valle Grande. Last time, it was stickers for Coco's skateboard. And the time before that, a hand-carved rattle for Baby Carlos, our little brother. This time, it's something for me.

I push the box into the living room, where Papi and Coco are putting on a puppet show for Carlos. Maybe they should audition for the talent show too.

"It's about time you got home," Coco says.

"We almost couldn't resist opening that box," Papi agrees.

Carlos claps his hands, all sticky with the applesauce he's been snacking on. I wrinkle my nose and make a mental note not to let him touch whatever's inside the package.

"Well, what are you waiting for?" Coco asks, leaping up from the carpet and flinging the dinosaur puppets off her hands. "Open it!"

Of course I'm going to open it. But first I need the proper tools. Calmly I carry my backpack to the coffee table and set it down. I unzip the middle pouch and take out my school scissors.

Coco groans.

Then I carefully snip the tape along one side of the box. I am about to move on to the next piece of tape when Coco nudges me aside.

"This is going to take forever!" she complains. She kneels beside the box and rips off the rest of the tape with one sharp tug. "There. It's open."

I want to tell Coco that patience makes perfect, but I am just as excited as she is to see what Tía Abuela sent. I lift open the cardboard flaps. The gift is wrapped in tissue paper, with a note card sitting on top.

I take the note card out of the box and read aloud, "Mi amiga Josefina tells me you are making excellent progress with your sewing. Keep practicing! Sewing can be like magic. But remember what I've told you. The magic is only as strong as your stitches."

I can imagine Tía Abuela winking behind her cat-eye sunglasses when she wrote those lines. I glance up to see if Papi or Coco suspect that Tía Abuela was writing about *real* magic. They don't, so I keep reading, "I wanted you to have some new material for your next projects. This fabric is from the fashion shows in Medellín. I can't wait to see what you create with it!"

I set the note card down and reach into the box. Underneath the tissue paper are bundles of fabric. Once piece is icy blue and speckled with silver stars. The largest piece is purple and satiny smooth. There's a zebra print—one of Tía Abuela's favorite patterns—and a piece that shimmers with pink and gold sequins.

Papi takes a velvety green square and uses it to play peekaboo with Carlos. I'm so dazzled by all the fabric that I don't even mind him touching it. *Much*.

"She didn't say anything else?" Papi asks after his next *Boo!* "Nothing about where she's traveling next?"

"I don't think so," I answer. She hardly ever does. Sometimes we try to guess where her next postcard will come from, but it's always a surprise. Papi should know that.

Then Coco picks up the note card. "She did! There's more writing on the back!"

I yank the note from her hand. Coco is right. I can't believe I missed it. Most of the time, I have excellent attention to detail. It's why Tía Abuela trusted me with the magic sewing kit in the first place. I read on, "Maybe you can show me what you're working on when I come to visit. Your papi told me you'll be singing in the school talent show. I wouldn't miss it! You know the old saying: 'Quien canta sus males espanta.' 'Whoever sings frightens their worries away.'"

"Is this true?" I ask when I get to the end.

Papi tilts his head and thinks for a moment. "Well, singing *does* put me in a good mood," he says. "So I suppose it's true."

"I'm not asking if the *saying* is true!" I reply. "I mean what Tía Abuela wrote before that. Is it true she's coming to visit?"

Papi laughs. "Surprise!" he says. "I knew Tía Abuela would love to hear you sing. Especially since you'll be performing one of her songs."

Coco takes the zebra-print fabric and whips it around her neck like a cape. "I can finally show her my kick flip!" she exclaims. "And Tía Abuela promised to bring back pictures of the big skate parks in South America."

Even Carlos starts to clap again.

Not me. I sit there, staring at the note.

"What's the matter, Kitty-Cat?" Papi asks. "Aren't you excited to see Tía Abuela?"

I can tell him at least one thing that's the matter: he won't stop calling me "Kitty-Cat." As I've told my family about a zillion times, I'm getting too old for all this kitten stuff.

But that's not *really* what's bothering me. *Of course* I'm excited to see Tía Abuela. I'm especially excited to show her how far my sewing has come. When she started to teach me over the summer, I could barely thread a needle.

But this news has made me even *more* nervous about the talent show audition. What if Banda La Chispa doesn't get picked for the show, and Tía Abuela travels all this way for nothing?

Or worse, what if we *do* get to perform, and we're terrible?

"I'm excited," I tell Papi finally. "But the band has a lot of practicing to do. *And* I need to get to Stitch and Share."

READ & LEARN

with *simon* kids

Keep your child reading, learning, and having fun with Simon Kids!

A one-stop shop where you can **find downloadable resources, watch interactive author videos, browse books by reading level, and more!**

Visit us at
SimonandSchusterPublishing.com/ReadandLearn/

And follow us @SimonKids

SIMON & SCHUSTER
Children's Publishing

Can DOMINGUITA learn to be the hero of her own adventures?

EBOOK EDITIONS AVAILABLE
Aladdin
simonandschuster.com/kids

Looking for another great book?
Find it
IN THE MIDDLE.

Fun, fantastic books for kids
in the in-be**TWEEN** age.

IntheMiddleBooks.com

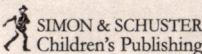   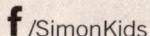 /SimonKids   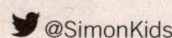 @SimonKids

Don't miss the Mindy Kim series!

ALADDIN | SIMON & SCHUSTER, NEW YORK
EBOOK EDITIONS ALSO AVAILABLE

Don't miss Catalina's other magical adventures!

The New Friend Fix
Off-Key

BY Jennifer Torres

CATALINA INCOGNITO

ILLUSTRATED BY
Gladys Jose

ALADDIN
New York London Toronto Sydney New Delhi

If you purchased this book without a cover, you should be aware that this book is stolen property. It was reported as "unsold and destroyed" to the publisher, and neither the author nor the publisher has received any payment for this "stripped book."

This book is a work of fiction. Any references to historical events, real people, or real places are used fictitiously. Other names, characters, places, and events are products of the author's imagination, and any resemblance to actual events or places or persons, living or dead, is entirely coincidental.

ALADDIN
An imprint of Simon & Schuster Children's Publishing Division
1230 Avenue of the Americas, New York, New York 10020
First Aladdin paperback edition March 2022
Text copyright © 2022 by Jennifer Torres
Illustrations copyright © 2022 by Gladys Jose
Also available in an Aladdin hardcover edition.
All rights reserved, including the right of reproduction in whole or in part in any form.
ALADDIN and related logo are registered trademarks of Simon & Schuster, Inc.
For information about special discounts for bulk purchases, please contact
Simon & Schuster Special Sales at 1-866-506-1949 or business@simonandschuster.com.
The Simon & Schuster Speakers Bureau can bring authors to your live event. For more
information or to book an event contact the Simon & Schuster Speakers Bureau
at 1-866-248-3049 or visit our website at www.simonspeakers.com.
Book designed by Laura Lyn DiSiena
The illustrations for this book were rendered digitally.
The text of this book was set in Century Schoolbook.
Manufactured in the United States of America 0623 OFF
4 6 8 10 9 7 5
Library of Congress Cataloging-in-Publication Data
Names: Torres, Jennifer, 1980- author. | Jose, Gladys, illustrator.
Title: Catalina incognito / by Jennifer Torres ; illustrated by Gladys Jose.
Description: First Aladdin paperback edition. | New York : Aladdin, 2022. |
Series: Catalina incognito ; book 1 | Audience: Ages 6 to 9. | Summary: Eight-year-old
Catalina Castañeda uses Tía Abuela's sewing kit to turn ordinary clothing into a magical
disguise, enabling her to uncover a thief at the local library.
Identifiers: LCCN 2021005136 (print) | LCCN 2021005137 (ebook) |
ISBN 9781534482791 (hc) | ISBN 9781534482784 (pbk) | ISBN 9781534482807 (ebook)
Subjects: CYAC: Disguise—Fiction. | Stealing—Fiction. | Persistence—Fiction. |
Magic—Fiction. | Great aunts—Fiction. | Hispanic Americans—Fiction.
Classification: LCC PZ7.1.T65 Cat 2022 (print) | LCC PZ7.1.T65 (ebook) | DDC [Fic]—dc23
LC record available at https://lccn.loc.gov/2021005136
LC ebook record available at https://lccn.loc.gov/2021005137

For my nana, Josephine, who taught me the magic of creativity

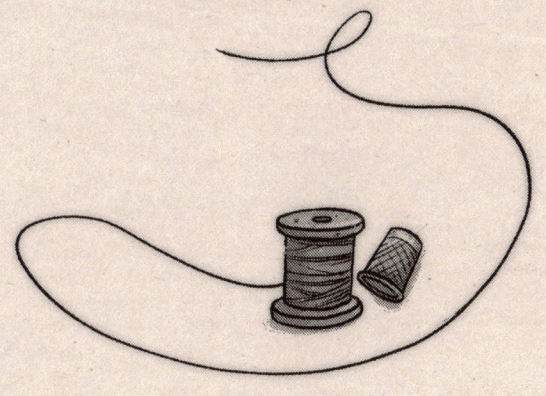

Contents

CHAPTER 1	Attention to Detail	1
CHAPTER 2	You Might Be Surprised	10
CHAPTER 3	Shoo	21
CHAPTER 4	The Basics	31
CHAPTER 5	The Big Reveal	39
CHAPTER 6	Incognito	50
CHAPTER 7	Long-Lost Twin	57
CHAPTER 8	Better Than Before	63
CHAPTER 9	Accidents Happen	70
CHAPTER 10	Secret Mission	76
CHAPTER 11	Clues	86
CHAPTER 12	Lost	95
CHAPTER 13	The Start	98
	Acknowledgments	105

CHAPTER 1

Attention to Detail

The picture on the puzzle box shows three gray kittens peeking out of a picnic basket.

Kittens. Of *course*.

If Mami and Papi didn't give me a kitten puzzle for my birthday, they would give me a kitten sticker collection. And if they didn't give me a kitten sticker collection, they would give me a kitten coloring book. Even though they know I am getting too old for all this kitten stuff. And even though I have told them to quit calling me "Kitty-Cat" and start using my real name, Catalina.

Everyone in my family—Mami and Papi; Baby Carlos in his high chair; my big sister, Coco; and Tía Abuela—is sitting around the kitchen table. They all lean forward, watching me.

"Well, Kitty-Cat," Papi asks, "what do you think?"

The first thing I think is, *Quit calling me "Kitty-Cat."*

But that's not what I say, because the *second* thing I think is that even though I don't love kittens as much as I used to, I still love puzzles. You get to figure out exactly where each piece belongs, and when you're finished, you know you haven't made any mistakes.

"It's perfect," I say.

"Maybe we can work on it together," Mami suggests.

Carlos claps. A droplet of drool drips off his lip and onto the high chair tray. I picture it landing on my puzzle. I fold my arms over the box to protect it from even the *idea* of Carlos's baby slobber.

"Hmm," I reply. Not quite a yes, and not exactly a no.

Luckily, Coco slides her gift across the table before I have to give a real answer.

She has wrapped it in this morning's newspaper. And lots and lots of tape. I don't have to open it to know what's inside—her old skateboard helmet.

"I'll even let you borrow my board," Coco says. She pulls the brim of her baseball cap lower down on her forehead. It hides her eyes, but not her smirk. "Unless you're still too scared after what happened the first time."

"I am *not* scared," I say, but my cheeks go warm as I remember last summer's wipeout.

Papi slaps his hands on the table. "Bravo, Coco!" he says. "Did you hear that, Kitty-Cat? Your sister is going to teach you to skateboard."

I don't need Coco to teach me, I think. This year I am ready. This year I will be perfect.

"Thank you, *Consuelo*," I say. I make my voice as sweet as a sip of horchata on a sunny afternoon. "You are *too* generous."

At last it is time to open Tía Abuela's gift. Tía Abuela's gifts are always the best.

Tía Abuela is Papi's aunt—my great-aunt—and her name is Catalina Castañeda too.

Only, most people know her as "La Chispa," the spark, one of the rottenest villains in telenovela history. Before she retired, the characters she played on TV were awfully, monstrously, fabulously *bad*. The rich but cruel stepmother. The beautiful but wicked duchess. The evil twin. Fans say her acting was so amazing, it was as if she *transformed* into every character.

Tía Abuela doesn't visit our house on the hill in Valle Grande very often. She's too busy traveling the world. But she always sends souvenirs home to my brother and sister and me.

Tía Abuela is only in town for the grand opening of the Catalina Castañeda Children's Room at the Valle Grande Central Library. The library was her favorite place to visit when she was growing up. It's where she first learned all about heroes and villains and adventures.

She's also here to celebrate my birthday, of course.

She has just returned from exploring the ancient Mayan city of Palenque in Mexico. Her gift comes in a box, wrapped in shimmering gold paper and a purple ribbon. I try to imagine what's inside. "An archaeologist's hand shovel?" I guess. "Ooh! I know, a map of the jungle!"

But when I untie the ribbon, tear apart the paper, and open the box, I don't find either of those things.

What I find instead is a red velvet pouch. It isn't new. Not even *almost* new. In fact, the pouch is so ancient, the cloth is worn bald in places.

It reminds me a little of an old dog with patchy fur. I try not to wrinkle my nose.

I know I should smile.

I know I should say "Thank you."

I know I should say *something*.

But I worry that if I so much as twitch, the groan I am trying to swallow will come tumbling out of my mouth before I can stop it.

"Not what you were expecting?" Tía Abuela says with a snort.

Not even close.

But it would be rude to just say so. So I don't.

I open the pouch and peer inside. There is a little brass thimble, a spool of silver thread, and a needle poking out of a strawberry-shaped pincushion.

Nope. Definitely not what I was expecting.

"Cata*lina* . . ." Mami nudges me with her voice. It's my name, but it is also a warning.

I try to think of something polite to say. "Thank you, Tía Abuela. It is so . . . so . . . so *different*."

Tía Abuela cackles. "Do you even know what it is, Kitty-Cat?"

I shake my head.

"It is a sewing kit. I've had it since I was your age. I thought it was the perfect gift for someone with your . . . How shall I put this?" She pauses. She taps a flamingo-pink fingernail against her lips as she thinks of the right thing to say. "Someone with your *attention to detail*. Attention to detail is very important when it comes to sewing."

"Hmm" is all I say.

• CHAPTER 2 •

You Might Be Surprised

Carlos whines and squirms until Papi lifts him out of the high chair and plops him onto the floor. Then Carlos crawls toward the living room—and straight for Tía Abuela's giant purse.

"Not so fast, señor." Tía Abuela yanks the bag away just as Carlos is about to tip it upside down. She carries it upstairs, her long pink fingernails clicking on the handrail as she climbs.

In the kitchen Papi fills the sink with sudsy

water. Coco and I help Mami stack the dirty dishes until we hear a *rrrrrrrooooolllSMACK* on the sidewalk outside.

Our heads snap up. Skateboards.

"Go ahead—" Mami starts to say. That's all Coco needs to hear. She races out the door before Mami can finish her sentence. Unfortunately, I am not as quick as Coco.

"But make sure you bring a sweatshirt," Mami continues.

A sweatshirt. Of *course*.

"But it's still summer vacation," I protest, even though I know it doesn't matter. Mami *always* makes us take a sweatshirt when we go outside after dinner. Even if it's August.

"It never hurts to be prepared," she says.

Ordinarily I'd agree. But not today. "I can't wear my sweatshirt," I say. "It's *ruined*."

Mami turns to me and puts her hands on her hips. "Kitty-Cat, don't be so quisquillosa."

"Kee-skee-YO-sah," Papi repeats slowly. As if I haven't heard the word about a million times before.

"That means 'persnickety,'" he adds. "And 'persnickety' means 'picky.'" As if I didn't already know.

"Your sweatshirt is *not* ruined," Mami continues. "The pocket is torn, that's all. It is still perfectly wearable. Now, you'd better go get it before you waste any more daylight arguing with me."

I stomp upstairs. I am *not* quisquillosa. Or persnickety. And that sweatshirt is definitely *not* perfect.

Not like my books, I think as I gaze at the shelves on my side of the bedroom. They are organized by color and by author.

Coco doesn't organize her books. They don't even face the same direction. Some stand upright. Some lie on their sides.

Some are *missing their covers*.

"They don't give trophies for neatest bookshelf, you know," Coco said once when I tried to give her some helpful tips.

Well, maybe they should. Because maybe then I'd get one. Carlos might be the cutest, and Coco might be the most courageous. But I'm definitely the most perfectly put together in the family.

Not that anyone gives me any credit for it.

I open my closet. Everything is right where it belongs.

Except my gray sweatshirt.

Its hanger, right between my sundress and my swimsuit (I like to keep my clothes alphabetical too), is empty.

I check the floor—spotless, as usual.

I peek behind the shoe rack. The sweatshirt's not there either.

I take a deep breath. I hold my nose. I prepare to search inside Coco's closet. I am about to fling open the door when Tía Abuela calls out from the guest room, "Kitty-Cat? Is that you?"

I let out my breath. "Coming, Tía Abuela."

I find her sitting in the rocking chair by the window. My gray sweatshirt is folded on her lap. The velvet sewing pouch she gave me rests on the nightstand. I didn't even notice her taking it upstairs.

Tía Abuela might not be on television anymore, but she still sparkles. She always wears cat-eye sunglasses with crystals on the frames, even indoors. Her lips are cherry red, and she has silver hair that falls in gentle waves.

"It's time for a sewing lesson," she says. "Estás lista?"

Am I ready? Outside the window the sun is sinking fast. Already the clouds are pinky-orange. "Hmm. I was going to skate with Coco," I try to explain. "But then Mami said I needed—"

"Tu chamarra?" Tía Abuela pats my sweatshirt. "I saw it was torn and thought you might like to fix it. Almost finished. Ven acá."

I do what she says and come closer, then kneel on the rug at her feet.

Tía Abuela lifts her sunglasses to her forehead, and I yelp. "AAAH!"

It looks like two black spiders are crawling on Tía Abuela's eyelids!

Then I realize, my heart still pounding, that those aren't spiders. They're just her lashes. Impossibly long false eyelashes.

Tía Abuela bats her eyes. "How do you like them?" she asks. "They're new."

I catch my breath. I try to think of something polite to say. "They are . . . so . . . so . . . *different*."

Tía Abuela chuckles. She takes the needle and spool of thread from the velvet pouch. "Just one last stitch," she says.

She pulls a long gold chain up from inside her

zebra-print blouse. At the end of the chain is a tiny pair of gold scissors.

Tía Abuela uses them to snip a length of thread off the spool. She squints and pokes the thread through the needle's eye.

"I didn't know you could sew," I say.

She rolls her eyes. "Por favor! Of course I can sew, Kitty-Cat. I made all my own costumes when I was starting out, you know."

"Even the Dragon Dress?" I ask.

The Dragon Dress is one of La Chispa's most famous costumes and also my favorite. It is a long, shimmering gown covered in emerald beads, with fiery orange sunstones and blazing-red rubies around the neck. Tía Abuela has donated the dress to the Valle Grande library. It will be on display at the grand opening tomorrow.

"Even the Dragon Dress," Tía Abuela says

proudly. "Including all the gems—seventy-five of them, each stitched on by hand. It took me weeks to finish."

She hands me the needle and thread.

"But I've never sewn before," I protest, trying to give them back. "I don't know how."

Tía Abuela rocks forward and back. "Coser y cantar, todo es empezar."

"Huh?" I understand a lot of Spanish words, but sometimes I need help.

"From sewing to singing, it's all about starting," Tía Abuela translates. "It's an old saying that means 'Whatever it is you are trying to do, the most important thing is just to begin.'"

She shows me how to tie a knot at the end of the thread and where to draw the needle through the fabric to close the last raw edge of the torn pocket.

"Sewing is like magic," she says as we finish.

"Take a piece of cloth, a bit of thread, and with a few stitches and some imagination, you can turn it all into something new."

She holds up the sweatshirt. "See? Magia!"

That's when I realize she has done more than fix the pocket. Tía Abuela has made two kitten ears and sewn them onto the hood, and added a diamond-shaped patch between them.

A kitten. Of course.

"How do you like it?" she asks.

I fight back a frown. "Gracias, Tía Abuela. Only—"

"You're getting too old for kittens?" Tía Abuela pulls her sunglasses back down over her eyes. The crystals twinkle. "Try it on. You might be surprised."

• CHAPTER 3 •

Shoo

There isn't time to take the ears off the hood now, not if I want to skateboard before it gets dark. I dash down the stairs and tear the newspaper wrapping off Coco's old helmet.

Once outside, I listen for the *whiiirrrrrCRACK* of wheels rolling over pavement, leaping the curb, and landing with a clatter on the sidewalk. When I hear it, I follow the sound to the end of the block, where Coco and her friends stand with their skateboards.

Coco's turn is next. I watch her tighten the smelly old plaid flannel shirt she always wears tied around her waist. Mami has bought her lots of new shirts, but Coco insists that *this* one is lucky. It's the one she was wearing when she landed her first trick.

She steps onto her skateboard with one foot and pushes off with the other. With one more push, she sails across the street. Just when it looks like she is about to crash for sure, she steps down hard on the back of the deck. The skateboard jumps up and over the curb. Everyone cheers as she comes down again and glides to a stop.

I drop my sweatshirt onto the sidewalk.

I buckle the helmet strap under my chin. "I'm ready."

Coco turns around. "Ready to stay on the board, I hope." She kicks up her skateboard and catches it under her arm. "Unlike last time?"

"Very funny," I say. Even though it is very *not*.

It happened last summer at the skate park. Coco stood on her skateboard, teetering over the edge of what looked like an empty swimming pool. Then she crouched, leaned forward, and rolled down the smooth wall, up the other side, and back down again. Even I could admit it was pretty amazing.

When I asked for a turn, Coco told me I should practice on some of the smaller ramps first.

But Coco was always treating me like a baby. And, anyway, it had looked so easy when she'd done it.

"Have it your way," she said finally. "But don't blame me when you wipe out."

I stood with the skateboard hanging over the edge of the bowl. Just like Coco. I crouched down. I leaned forward. So far, so good . . . until the wheels slipped. I flung out my arms, trying to catch my balance. But it was too late. The skateboard rolled down the wall. And I went tumbling down behind it.

I haven't ridden a skateboard since then, but I have been watching Coco all summer. I have memorized every move. I will land the trick even more perfectly than she can. No mistakes.

I grab Coco's skateboard and set it on the ground in front of me.

"Fine, Cat," Coco says. "But you'd better borrow my kneepads too. I don't want to get in trouble when you go home full of bruises."

I am not going to go home full of bruises. I am going to go home a skating *star*. But I put the kneepads on anyway. I step on the board with one foot and push off with the other. Exactly like Coco. *Better* than Coco.

"Just take it slow at first, okay?" she says.

That only makes me push even harder. The skateboard speeds up. *I am doing it!* I think.

I fly faster and faster. The curb comes closer and closer.

Too close.

I jump off and stumble backward as the skateboard slams into the curb.

"Cat!" Coco yells, jogging over to check on her board.

Her friends laugh.

I yank off the helmet and Coco's pads, then run across the street for my sweatshirt. If only there hadn't been so many people watching, if only Coco didn't always treat me like a baby, I *know* I could have done it.

"Cat!" Coco calls after me again. I don't turn around. All I want to do is hide. So even though it isn't chilly outside—not even close—I put on my sweatshirt, zip it up to my chin, and pull the hood low over my forehead.

A chill runs down my back and straight to the tips of my fingers and toes. *Strange*, I think as I start walking again.

Mami is sweeping the front porch when I get home. She looks up when I start climbing the steps.

"Where do you think you're going? Shoo!" Mami says, waving the broom at me.

I dodge and try to go around her.

Mami steps in front of me. She blocks the door. She can't stand it when we track dirt inside, especially after she's just swept. But I *always* take my shoes off first. Unlike Coco.

"Oh, no you don't," Mami says. She backs into the house and slams the screen shut. "Shoo, Cat. Go away."

And she calls *me* persnickety.

I walk around to the side door that opens into the laundry room. I step out of my shoes, unzip my sweatshirt, and wriggle out of it.

In the kitchen Mami is emptying the dustpan into a wastebasket. Tía Abuela sits at the table with a book, *Useful Knots for the New Sailor*. In a few days she will leave Valle Grande to sail far away to the Galápagos Islands. Her sunglasses are pushed down to the very tip of her nose. She looks over them as she reads.

"Catalina," Mami says, "what have we told you

about feeding stray cats? When you feed them, they think they belong to us."

I don't know what she's talking about. "I haven't been feeding any strays," I say as I fill a glass with water.

"Oh, no? Then why did a cat just stroll up the front steps like she lived here?"

Now I'm even more confused. "I was outside a second ago," I say. "I didn't see any cats."

Tía Abuela glances up from her book. "What did the cat look like?"

"Gray," Mami says. "With a patch of white fur on her forehead. Like a diamond."

I almost spit out the water I gulped. That sounds almost exactly like—

Tía Abuela interrupts my thought. "Gray with a diamond-shaped patch of fur on her forehead?" she repeats. "You don't see that every day."

She looks at the sweatshirt draped over my arm, then straight into my eyes. She winks. Her spidery eyelashes flutter.

I swallow another drink of water.

Mami shakes her head. "No, I guess not. But the cat did look very familiar. I'm sure I've seen her before. . . . Anyway, the point is, I don't want you girls feeding animals. You're the only Kitty-Cat who's welcome around here, comprendes?"

I'm not sure I *do* understand, but I nod anyway.

Tía Abuela closes her book. "Kitty-Cat, I think you're ready for another sewing lesson."

· CHAPTER 4 ·

The Basics

Tía Abuela leads me to the guest room. She points to the edge of her bed, inviting me to sit.

But I can't sit. I can't even close my mouth.

"Don't look so sorprendida," Tía Abuela says. "Didn't I tell you sewing is like magic?"

"Surprised" is an understatement. "You didn't tell me it was *that* kind of magic. *Real* magic."

"Would you have believed me if I had?" she asks.

Probably not. In fact, I don't quite believe her

now. "You're saying the sewing kit . . . turned me into a cat?"

Tía Abuela clicks her tongue. "Por favor! Kitty-Cat, don't you think you would *know* if you had turned into a cat?"

I don't *feel* like a cat, but I look over my shoulder just in case. No tail. No fur.

Tía Abuela snorts.

"So, it just made Mami *think* I was a cat? Like a disguise?"

"Un disfraz. Sí, something like that," Tía Abuela agrees. "The person who wears the disguise must tie the last knot to seal the spell. Pero none of that matters if you don't know how to sew. The magic is only as strong as your stitches."

When I first unwrapped Tía Abuela's sewing kit, I didn't know what to do with it. Now ideas race through my mind so fast, I almost can't keep up with them.

I remember Coco's flannel shirts. Maybe I could turn one of them into a skater disfraz to trick Coco and her friends into taking me seriously.

"I know what to make!" I spring off the bed. "I'll be right back."

But Tía Abuela holds up a hand to stop me. Her gold bangles clink as they slide down her wrist. "Not so fast, señorita. First you need to learn the basics. Mi bolsa, por favor."

The basics? This is just like Coco making me start with the baby ramps at the skate park. I sigh and retrieve Tía Abuela's purse from the other side of the room. It is heavier than it looks.

She rummages through her bag, then pulls out a blue cookie tin. *Perfect*, I think. *I could use a snack.* Except instead of cookies inside, there are needles, thread, safety pins, and buttons.

"More sewing supplies?" I ask, trying not to

sound too disappointed. I guess *nothing* is what it appears to be.

"Sí. These ones are for everyday projects," she says. "Just what we need for practice. Primero, we thread the needle."

Tía Abuela holds up a needle, and the light from her reading lamp shines through its eye. She nods at me to make sure I'm paying attention. I nod back to show her I am.

Next she unspools some thread and snips it with her tiny gold scissors. She pinches one end of the thread between her thumb and pointer finger, squints, sticks out her tongue, and pokes the thread straight through the needle's eye.

Then she pulls the thread out again. "Now you try."

I pinch the thread between my thumb and finger. Just like Tía Abuela. I hold the needle up to the light and squint. I even stick out my tongue.

I aim . . . and miss.

I try again.

And then again.

My shoulders slump. "I'll never be any good at this." I let the needle and thread fall to my lap. Tía Abuela doesn't look up. She just sits in the rocking chair, stitching on a scrap of fabric.

"Qué lástima," she says, shaking her head. "What a shame to waste all that magic."

I think about Coco's flannel and try again.

And again.

At last the thread slides through the needle's eye.

"Finally!"

"Sí, por fin," Tía Abuela repeats. "Now we can move on to the running stitch." She shows me the neat dashed line she has sewn along the edge of the fabric scrap, then hands it to me. "Your turn."

As Tía Abuela teaches me how to pull the thread—over, under, over, under—through the fabric, she tells me how she, too, received the red velvet sewing pouch on her eighth birthday.

"Pero, *I* did a better job of pretending to like it," she adds. "Of course, I was an actress, even then."

It was a gift from her mami, another Catalina, who had received it from *her* mami before that. "It's amazing how many problems you can solve with a needle and thread," she continues. "And not just rips and tears. My great-grandmother used hers to sew banners to rally for the right to vote. And her grandmother before that sewed a disguise to sneak into university classes when women were not allowed there. I wonder what you will create."

It sounds so important all of a sudden. "Why

did you give the sewing kit to *me*?" I ask. "Why not Papi?" I scowl. "Or . . . Coco?"

Tía Abuela pauses before answering. "I thought about that, but I needed someone more . . ." She taps her fingernail against her lips.

"Careful?" I suggest. "Orderly? Perfectly put together?"

Tía Abuela shakes her head. "Quisquillosa," she says. "And that's why it's your turn to keep the magic safe. We all start out with a fresh spool of thread, but remember, when your thread is gone, it's gone forever. So only use it when you really need it."

I finish my first row of stitches. Next to Tía Abuela's, they are crooked, uneven, loose. Not perfect. Not in order. Not even close.

"What a *mess*."

Tía Abuela leans over for a closer look. She lifts up her glasses. "Sí," she agrees.

I groan. "I wanted them to be perfect."

"Pues, they might never be *perfectos*," Tía Abuela says. "But they will be a little bit better each time you try."

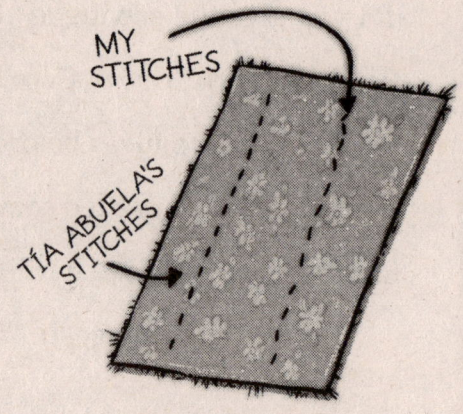

There is a gentle knock on the door. Papi peeks into the room. "Kitty-Cat?" he says. "Time to get some sleep. Tomorrow is a big day."

Tía Abuela winks at me. "Shoo, Kitty-Cat," she says. "I'll see you por la mañana."

But when I wake up the next morning, Tía Abuela isn't there.

• CHAPTER 5 •

The Big Reveal

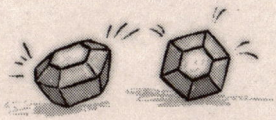

Tía Abuela doesn't answer when I knock on the guest room door. She isn't in the kitchen when I go downstairs to pour myself a bowl of cereal.

Only Papi is at the table, sipping his coffee and grading math exams from the summer school class he teaches at Valle Grande Community College.

"Where's Tía Abuela?"

"She walked down to the library already," he

says, glancing up from his work. "She wanted to get there early to make sure everything is ready for the grand opening."

I smile to myself. *Finally. Someone else who understands the importance of punctuality.* I only wish Tía Abuela had taken me with her.

After breakfast I go back upstairs to get dressed—and to plan my first sewing project.

Coco is still snoring softly on the top bunk. I reach up and poke her foot, then wait to see if she stirs. When she doesn't, I creep to her closet and snatch a plaid flannel shirt from the heap on the floor. Tía Abuela said to save the magic for when I really need it. After dreaming about skateboarding most of the night, I'm sure I *really* do.

Suddenly Coco rolls over and mumbles something. Sounds that aren't exactly words.

I stand perfectly still. I hold my breath.

When Coco starts snoring again, I hang her shirt up in my closet. She'll never even notice it's missing.

"We're going to be late," I warn my family for the eleventh time that day. I am pacing in front of the door, waiting to leave for the library.

"Kitty-Cat, you are being impatient," Papi says.

"And irritating," Coco grumbles.

By the time we finally walk down the hill to the library, a crowd has gathered inside the lobby. Standing front and center is a boy wearing a white guayabera and khaki pants. He holds an autograph book in one hand, a pen in the other.

I groan. "Pablo Blanco."

Pablo is my only real rival at Valle Grande Elementary. He's also sort of my friend. No one else in our class—or even our school—has our attention to detail.

Pablo's spelling is more precise. But my cursive is more impeccable.

I always stay late after school to make sure the whiteboards are wiped completely clean. Pablo arrives early to check that the clocks aren't running too fast or too slow.

I am La Chispa's grand-niece. He is La Chispa's number one fan.

But that doesn't mean he's allowed to touch the Dragon Dress.

The gown is in the middle of the lobby, hidden behind black curtains until the big reveal. As fans crowd into the room, Pablo inches closer and closer to the dress. He pulls back an edge of the curtain.

"Don't touch that!" I shout.

Pablo jumps. He looks at me and frowns.

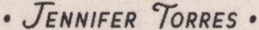

"Catalina Castañeda," he says. He drops the curtain and buries one hand in his pocket. The other hand still clutches his autograph book and pen. He looks like he is about to argue, but then his eyes widen at something behind me.

I spin around. Josefina the Librarian and Tía Abuela have just stepped into the lobby. Tía Abuela wears a gold-studded jacket over black leather pants. The crystals on her sunglasses twinkle.

Pablo rushes toward her, holding out his pen and autograph book.

Tía Abuela laughs as she takes them from him.

"Por favor! Not another one, Pablo," she says. But she signs her name anyway.

She closes the book and hands it back.

"Una foto?" he asks.

Tía Abuela grins and tosses her silver waves. "Anything for my number one fan."

But before Pablo can take a picture, Josefina clears her throat. She looks down at her watch. Even from a distance I can tell it's the same one she always wears, silver with a cat's face on the front. The minute and hour hands look like whiskers. I used to wish I had one just like it. *Used* to, but not anymore.

"Oh," Tía Abuela says. "Is it time?" She strides to the center of the room, her high-heeled boots clacking against the floor tiles.

Josefina clears her throat again. Then, reading

from note cards, she tells the story of Tía Abuela's famous telenovela past.

"And now," Josefina the Librarian says, wrapping up, "it is my pleasure to dedicate the new Valle Grande Central Library children's room in honor of our generous patron, Catalina Castañeda."

Tía Abuela holds a hand over her heart. "Por favor, you can call me 'La Chispa.'"

Everyone cheers. Josefina the Librarian flips to another note card. "To mark the occasion," she goes on, "Catalina—La Chispa—has donated the 'Dragon Dress,' which she wore in . . ."

She shuffles the cards. "Which she wore in . . ."

Pablo stands on tiptoe. He raises his hand way up like when he's trying to answer a question in class.

"Which she wore in . . ."

"*A Heart of Fire!*" Pablo finally blurts.

"Yes, of course," Josefina the Librarian says.

"Which she wore in *A Heart of Fire*. Now, Catalina, will you do the honors?"

Tía Abuela whisks the curtains back and reveals the shimmering emerald gown.

Everyone cheers again.

"Magnífico!" Pablo sighs.

"A little much," Josefina mutters.

"It's *ruined*!" I yell.

A moment ago, everyone was staring at the Dragon Dress. Now they all whip their heads around to stare at me.

"Kitty-Cat?" Tía Abuela asks.

I push my way to the front. "Ruined," I say again. I point to the collar. I can't believe no one else has noticed the small empty space. "See? A ruby is missing. There."

Curious whispers buzz around the room.

"Missing? Por favor! Of course not," Tía Abuela

says. She laughs nervously and steps in front of the gown. "Everything is right where it belongs."

I check again, just to be sure.

And I'm *sure*. "No," I insist. "Look closer."

Visitors lean in. Some begin to point.

"It is a very old dress, Kitty-Cat," Tía Abuela says. "Maybe one of the stones just . . . popped off."

Impossible. I have seen Tía Abuela sew. Her

stitches are straight and strong. The ruby could *not* have just popped off.

I am about to say so when, out of the corner of my eye, I notice Pablo leaving the library.

"Hey, wait!" I call out. But he doesn't stop.

· CHAPTER 6 ·

Incognito

Tía Abuela stays at the library awhile longer to sign autographs. I can't stop thinking about the missing ruby as the rest of us walk home that afternoon.

"I wish I knew who had that missing ruby," I say.

No one answers. We walk past four more houses. "I wonder if we will *ever* find that missing ruby."

"Kitty-Cat, this is getting tedious," Mami complains.

"And tiresome," adds Papi. "If Tía Abuela isn't

worried about it, you shouldn't be either. Try to let it go."

But I can't. Someone has ruined Tía Abuela's most famous costume. Now the only thing I'll ever see when I look at the Dragon Dress is the empty space where a ruby should sparkle. It's like a puzzle with a piece missing, which is the worst thing that can happen to a puzzle. Even worse than baby slobber.

No matter what she says, Tía Abuela must be upset about what's happened. I have to get that ruby back before she leaves.

And I know just where to start looking.

I burst through the front door as soon as Mami opens it. I don't take off my shoes first. I don't even stomp the dust off. I run upstairs and open my closet. I shove aside Coco's flannel—the disfraz will have to wait—and grab my gray sweatshirt. *That* gray sweatshirt.

"I'm going to visit Pablo," I say as I scramble back down the stairs.

"Sure thing, Kitty-Cat," Mami says. "But don't forget to take a—"

"Sweatshirt," I say as I'm stepping out the door. "I know."

Halfway down the block, I hide behind a trash bin. When I am sure no one is looking, I slip my arms into the sweatshirt and zip it up to my chin. I pull the hood over my head and feel a shiver flutter down my spine. That must mean I am incognito. Disguised, I scurry to Pablo's house.

It's easy to tell which window is his. It's the cleanest. No spots, no streaks. I borrow a basketball from the neighbor's yard and carefully climb on top of it to peek inside Pablo's room.

I'm so startled when I see my reflection in the window that I nearly tumble off the ball. Staring back at me is a gray cat with sleek fur and long, silky whiskers. *Purrr-fectly put together*, I think.

But I can't just stand here admiring myself. I look past my reflection and into the room. No one is inside. The first thing I notice is Pablo's bookshelf. He has organized his books, not just by color but also by . . . height?

I shake my head. *Focus*, I remind myself.

I press my nose against the window. Framed photographs, some of Tía Abuela and some of other actors, are arranged on top of Pablo's desk. Autographed posters hang on the walls. An enormous silver belt buckle gleams from inside its own display case. The buckle must have been a prop on one of those telenovelas set on an old rancho.

But I don't see the ruby. Not even a twinkle of it.

Pablo's door opens, and I dip my head. When I poke it up again, Pablo is standing at his desk. He reaches into his pocket for something. Could it be the gem?

Before I can get a closer look, the basketball rolls under my feet. I grasp at the windowsill, trying to steady myself, but the ball spins away. "AAH!" I scream, but it comes out like a kitten's yowl. I land on the ground, hard enough to shake the hood off my head.

The window opens.

Pablo sticks his head out. He looks left. He looks right.

He looks down.

"Oh," he says. "It's just you. Catalina Castañeda." He glances left and right again. "I thought I saw a cat out here. I'm allergic. *And* I didn't want its dirty paws on my windows. I just cleaned them this morning."

I stand and dust off my leggings. "Really? This morning? You know, you left some streaks."

Pablo scowls. "You know, there's dirt all over your nose."

I turn away from him and swipe my face with my sleeve. Then I narrow my eyes. "You sure left the library in a hurry. It didn't have anything to do with the missing ruby, did it?"

Pablo leans out the window. "Of course it did."

CHAPTER 7
Long-Lost Twin

Has Pablo actually confessed?

"Give it back, then," I demand.

Pablo crosses his arms over his chest. "Give what back?"

"The ruby from the Dragon Dress, of course," I tell him. "You just admitted you took it."

"Me?" He gasps. "Damage one of the most important costumes in telenovela history? Nunca." *Never.* He shudders. "But I think I know who did. I came

straight home to be sure. Hold on a minute."

Pablo ducks back into his room and returns with a black scrapbook. He hands it down to me. "Don't you see? This is *just* like what happened in the telenovela *My Sister, the Stranger*. I've been trying to explain it to my mom, but she thinks it's just a coincidence."

I flip through the scrapbook. Each page is filled with pictures and articles cut out of old magazines. I don't understand what Pablo is talking about. "You're not trying to distract me, are you?" I ask. "Throw me off the trail?"

Pablo shakes his head. "Move over," he says. "I'll explain."

I step back as Pablo swings his legs out the window and hops down. He lands on his feet. Just like a cat.

Of *course*.

Pablo snatches back the scrapbook and opens it to a page near the end.

"Here," he says, holding the page open for me to see. He points to a black-and-white picture of Tía Abuela taken when she was about Papi's age. She looks dangerous, with arching eyebrows and snarling lips.

There's another picture right next to it. It's of Tía Abuela too, only I don't recognize her at first. She looks friendlier in this one, with a sunny smile and a dimple in each cheek.

I start to read the caption aloud. "Paulina Mendez has it all: a perfect house, a perfect job, a perfect family—"

Pablo closes his eyes and recites the rest of the words by heart:

"Until a stranger comes to town—Paulina's long-lost twin, who is determined to steal everything Paulina loves."

He opens his eyes and looks at me as if that explains everything.

It does not.

"So Tía Abuela was playing twin sisters," I say. "What does that have to do with the missing ruby?"

"Ugh." Pablo flips to another page. "Here."

It is Tía Abuela again, only much younger. In this picture she is laughing, her arm around another girl's shoulders.

"I feel like I've seen that girl before," I say. "But I don't know where."

Pablo rolls his eyes. "Just *read*."

"Catalina Castañeda and Josefina Chavez star as mischievous twins in *Double Trouble*."

Pablo taps the picture of Josefina with his finger.

"*Now* do you understand? Josefina the Librarian starred in a telenovela too—with La Chispa. But that was Josefina's first and only role. She could never be a star. She must have gotten jealous over the years. So jealous that she decided to ruin La Chispa's big moment *and* her most famous costume."

I roll up my sweatshirt sleeves and lean against the side of Pablo's house to think. I try to remember everything that happened at the library this afternoon.

"I guess Josefina did seem a little impatient," I say.

Still, I am not convinced that Pablo hasn't stolen the ruby himself. Finding out Josefina has it would be one way to know for sure.

"I'm going back to the library to check it out," I say. "And you're coming with me." I can't risk letting him out of my sight.

"Of course I am," Pablo says. He stands on tiptoe

to drop the scrapbook back through his bedroom window. "*You* wouldn't know how to take care of the ruby if you found it."

We both look down at our watches. "Too late," we say at the same time.

"It's 5:01," Pablo says.

"It's 5:01 and thirty-seven seconds," I correct him. "The library closed at five. But it opens again tomorrow at ten a.m. Don't be late."

• CHAPTER 8 •

Better Than Before

Walking back home, I hear the roll and smack of Coco's skateboard on the sidewalk.

Then I hear new sounds: *Thud.*

"Uf! Ow!"

I run ahead and find Coco sitting on the curb. She is rubbing her shoulder.

"Are you okay?"

Coco looks up. "You didn't just see that."

"No," I say. "I heard it, though."

Coco pushes the skateboard toward me. It rolls to my feet. "You should try again," she says.

I push it back to her with the toe of my sneaker. She just wants to see me *fall* again. "No way."

Coco wipes her palms on her flannel shirt, still tied around her waist. Then she holds out her arms like Baby Carlos does when he wants to be carried.

"Fine. Help me up."

I grab Coco's hands and pull. "What happened? You never fall."

"I fall all the time when I'm learning a new trick," she admits. She tightens the helmet strap under her chin. "But this time I'm going to land it. I can feel it."

I can't believe what I'm hearing. "You're not actually going to do that again, are you?" I ask. "Aren't you scared you'll mess up?"

Coco shrugs. "If I'm afraid to mess up, I'll lose my chance to get better." She hops back onto her skateboard.

I step out of her way.

Coco pushes down with her back foot and jumps up with the other as the board spirals underneath her.

For a split second she hangs in the air, and I think, *She's doing it!*

But when Coco comes back down, the board skids out from under her, and she thumps to the sidewalk again. I cringe. I expect her to scream. Instead she smiles. "That was my best one yet!" Then she holds out her arms again. "Help."

I pull Coco to her feet and glance down at the skateboard. If she can get that excited about falling, it might be worth another try after all.

"Maybe . . ." But no. I can't do it. "Never mind."

"Why not?" Coco unbuckles her helmet and lifts

it off. "Don't tell anyone I said this, but you didn't do that bad the other day."

"I didn't?"

She shakes her head. "No. You were way better than that time at the skate park. I bet you stayed on the board a whole five seconds. Think you can make it to six?" She tosses the helmet to me.

I catch it but don't put it on. "Some other time," I reply. Standing on a skateboard for six seconds doesn't seem like much, especially compared to what Coco can do. "After I've watched you some more. Then I'll be ready."

I try to give the helmet back, but Coco pushes it toward me again.

"Come on, Cat. You won't start to get better until you . . . *start*."

It reminds me of what Tía Abuela said about sewing. About how, whether it's sewing or singing—

or skateboarding—the most important thing is to begin.

"Well . . ." I look around. It's only me and my sister. No one else is watching. "Maybe just one more time."

Coco pumps her fist. "Yes!" She picks up the skateboard and positions it in front of me. "Now, bend your knees a little. That will help you balance."

I step on top of the board. It wobbles underneath my feet, and I fling my arms out to steady myself. "Whoa."

"Bend," Coco reminds me.

I nod and bend my knees. She's right! I don't feel like I'm about to topple over anymore. I pick up my back leg and get ready to give myself a giant push.

"Wait!" Coco yells.

"Wait?" I thought she wanted me to start. I put my foot on the ground and look up at her.

"Take it slow."

This time I listen. I push gently off my back foot, and the skateboard rolls forward. With me still on top of it.

Coco starts counting. "One! Two! Three!"

I'm not slipping. I'm not stumbling. I'm staying on! I count along with her. "Four! Five!"

When we get to six, I jump off the board and spin around. Coco is already running toward me. "You did it!" She raises her hand for a high five.

I might not be better than Coco. But I'm definitely better than before. I slap her hand, and we walk the rest of the way home together.

· CHAPTER 9 ·

Accidents Happen

Onions sizzle in a frying pan, and steam curls over a pot. "Dinner will be ready in half an hour," Papi says as Coco and I step into the kitchen. "Why don't you two wash up?"

Baby Carlos sits on the floor, surrounded by pots and pans. He smacks a wooden spoon against a metal mixing bowl. *Clang, clang, clang.*

I kneel down to ruffle his feathery brown hair.

He gurgles, then grabs one of the kitten ears on

my sweatshirt. He clutches it in his fist and pulls it toward his mouth.

"No, no, Carlos." I shake the sweatshirt gently, trying to loosen it from his hands.

But Carlos won't let go. His grip only tightens.

I pick up a set of measuring spoons and jangle them in front of his nose. Carlos bats the spoons away. He tugs on my hood again, this time with both hands.

I tug too until . . . *Rrrrriiip.*

"Uh-oh," Carlos says. He lets go of the ear and lets it drop to the floor.

"Carlos, no! My sweatshirt! It's—" I am about to say "ruined." Papi stops stirring the onions and waits for me to finish.

"It's . . . something I can fix," I say instead.

"Bravo," Papi says. "Good attitude, Kitty-Cat. Accidents happen." He goes back to stirring the onions. Carlos goes back to drumming on the mixing bowl.

It might be true that accidents happen, but this one could not have happened at a worse time. If I'm going to investigate Josefina the Librarian, I'm going to need to sneak into her office. And if I'm going to sneak into her office, I'm going to need a disfraz. A good one.

I take the sweatshirt, the loose kitten ear, and the red velvet sewing pouch to Tía Abuela's room.

She is reading again—a book called *Fashion for*

the High Seas. I hate to interrupt her, but this is urgent. "Can we have another sewing lesson?" I hold the sweatshirt in one hand and the scrap of fabric that used to be a kitten ear in the other.

Tía Abuela closes her book and sets it on the nightstand.

"Qué pasó, Kitty-Cat?" she asks.

"Carlos happened." I flop down onto the bed.

Tía Abuela sits next to me. "Well, go on, then," she says. "Let's see if you remember how to thread a needle."

I open the pouch and pull the needle from the strawberry pincushion. I unwind a little of the silvery thread and tear it between my teeth. I aim. I squint. And . . . I miss.

But this time I don't get discouraged. I imagine Coco stepping back onto her skateboard even after she falls. I try again, slow and steady, and the thread slips through the needle's eye.

"Bravo! You're getting better already." Tía Abuela pats my shoulder.

"I think I am!" I agree. But knowing how long it will take to get as good as she is makes me even more upset about the Dragon Dress.

"Doesn't it bother you that someone stole the ruby and spoiled all your hard work?"

Tía Abuela twirls one of the gold bangles around her wrist. "How do you know it was stolen?"

I think about Pablo and how much he'd probably love to add a piece of the Dragon Dress to his collection.

I think about Josefina and how badly she might have wanted to steal Tía Abuela's spotlight.

But I don't have any proof. Yet.

"You don't *really* think it just popped off on its own, do you?"

"Hmm," Tía Abuela replies. Not quite a yes, but not exactly a no. She changes the subject. "Are you going to fix that sweatshirt, or what?" She holds the kitten ear against the sweatshirt hood. "Unless . . ."

She pauses and pulls out her tiny gold scissors. "Didn't you say you were getting too old for kittens? Maybe you would rather snip both ears off instead?"

"No! I *need* . . . I mean, I *want* the ears. You were right. The sweatshirt was missing something." I wink—just like Tía Abuela does—and we get to work.

· CHAPTER 10 ·

Secret Mission

The next morning I get to the library at exactly 9:55 and forty-six seconds. My sweatshirt, with both ears sewn on, is tucked under my arm.

Pablo is already waiting at the entrance. He taps his toe against the pavement. When he sees me, he looks down at his watch. "You're almost late," he says. Behind me Mami is towing Baby Carlos down the hill in a red wagon. Coco rolls alongside them on her skateboard. "And you brought company. I thought this was a *secret* mission."

"Couldn't help it."

When I asked Mami if I could walk down to the library this morning, she insisted on coming along. "Carlos loves Baby Story Time," she said. "And my shift at the nursing home doesn't start until this afternoon." Plus, it's Coco's day to volunteer with the summer reading club, so Mami thought we should all walk together.

She parks the wagon. "See, Kitty-Cat, I told you it was too early," she says. "The library isn't even open yet."

Pablo steps toward her. "You know what they say, Señora Castañeda, 'El que madruga coge la oruga.' The early bird catches the worm."

Then he leans toward me and whispers, "But *we're* here to catch a jewel thief."

"Shh," I hiss. By now there are almost a dozen

people waiting for the library to open. "Someone will hear you."

Finally Josefina the Librarian unlocks the doors. Visitors step aside to let Mami roll the wagon in. Carlos gurgles and claps. Coco leaves her skateboard just inside the entrance.

Pablo and I let everyone else file past us.

"So, what's our plan?" he asks, his voice low.

I figured it all out last night. "Here's what we're going to do: I'll ask Josefina if I can help her shelve books. She'll go get the cart. That's your signal. When she comes back, get her to follow you to the history section. It's usually pretty empty there. And then *I'll* sneak into her office to look for the ruby."

"But what about the 'Staff Only' doors?" he asks. "They're always locked."

"Just leave it to me," I say.

Pablo's eyes flash. "This is *exactly* like what happened in the final episode of *Casa Misteriosa*." Then he notices my sweatshirt. "You know it's August, right? You're not *cold*, are you?"

I raise one eyebrow. "It's like my tía abuela says, 'You might be surprised.'"

We go inside. Josefina and her assistant, Ernest, are arranging cushions around a rainbow-colored rug for Baby Story Time. Mami sits down, but she has to get right back up when Carlos crawls away toward a shelf of alphabet books.

I lean against a magazine rack and look around.

A few steps away, a boy plunks three books down onto the reference desk, and Coco stamps his summer reading passport.

Some older kids sit at a study table, flipping through comics. Nearby, people sit down at the computer stations. The keyboards *click, click, click* as they type.

• CATALINA INCOGNITO •

In the middle of it all, the Dragon Dress is on display behind velvet ropes. My eyes zoom to the ugly empty space where that ruby should sparkle.

I reach for a magazine. *Kittens Today*.

Of course.

I turn the pages, pretending to read them, until I see Josefina walking toward me.

"I see you found our newest subscription," she says. "I ordered it just for you. We cat lovers need to look out for each other."

Quickly I put the magazine back on the rack. "Gracias," I say, "but I don't really . . ." I am about to say I don't really like all that cat stuff anymore. But there isn't time to waste. I have a mission.

"Yes?" Josefina asks.

"I mean, I don't really . . . want to look at magazines right now. Do you have any books I can help put away?"

Josefina smiles. "Wait here. I'll go get the cart."

I knew she wouldn't suspect a thing. Shelving books—putting them back *exactly* where they belong—is pretty much my favorite thing to do at the library.

Pablo peers out from behind the biographies. I nod at him.

"Here you go, Catalina," Josefina says when she returns with the cart. "Why don't you start with—"

Right on time as always, Pablo interrupts us. "Señora Josefina!" he shouts, coming up behind her. "I have been looking all over for you."

Josefina jumps. She clutches the cat-shaped turquoise pendant she always wears. "Pablo Blanco," she says. "What have I told you about sneaking up on people like that? I'll be with you in a moment. I am just—"

He doesn't let her finish.

"But this is *important*," Pablo insists. "My mom and I just started watching *Doña Laura, the Scholar* last night, and now I need to find out everything there is to know about the National University of San Marcos. It's a real place, you know. In Peru."

Josefina the Librarian looks from Pablo to me and

back to Pablo. "Yes, I know it's a real place, Pablo," she says. "We can start in the South American history section if you'll wait just a—"

"South American history?" Pablo says. "Vamos!" *Let's go.* He takes Josefina's wrist and leads her to the other side of the library.

"Don't worry, Señora Josefina." I wave. "I know what to do."

As they disappear behind the shelves, I make sure the coast is clear. Baby Story Time has just started. Mami and Carlos clap along as Ernest strums a guitar. The boy with the reading passport is searching for new books. The older kids are still reading their comics.

With everyone distracted, I wheel the cart down the hallway and crouch behind it.

I unfold my sweatshirt and remember Tía Abuela's warning. *The magic is only as strong as your stitches.* My stitches are still not as straight as Tía Abuela's. But I hope they're strong enough.

I push my arms through the sleeves and zip the sweatshirt up to my chin. A chill runs down my back as I pull the hood over my head. I am incognito.

CHAPTER 11

Clues

Using the library cart as a shield, I creep toward the history section. I don't want anyone to see me before Josefina does.

Just as I predicted, she and Pablo are the only ones here. "You might also be interested in Peruvian music," Josefina is saying as she adds another book to the stack in Pablo's arms. "And maybe food."

This is my chance. I slip out from behind the cart.

Pablo sees me first. His nose begins to twitch. "Cat?"

I freeze, worried he has recognized me. But then Pablo drops all the books he's holding right in time to cover a gigantic sneeze.

Achoo!

"Salud," Josefina says, stretching to pull a book off the top shelf. "Did you say 'cats'? Animal books are in a completely different section, Pablo."

"NO!" he says, pointing. "Cat!" *Achoo!* "Right there! I can't even"—*Achoo!*—"look at them without sneezing."

He races to the other side of the library.

Josefina bends down. "Well, hello there," she says. "How did you get in?"

She reaches out to pat my head, and I skitter away. I'm not *really* a cat, after all, and I don't know what might happen if she touches me.

"You're shy," Josefina says. "That's all 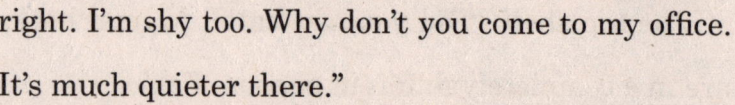 right. I'm shy too. Why don't you come to my office. It's much quieter there."

"Perfecto!" I shout. Only, it comes out like a purr. I trot behind Josefina as she leads the way across the library and down the hall. She waves a badge at the STAFF ONLY doors to unlock them, and we step right through.

I follow Josefina to her office, and she switches on the lights. "Make yourself at home," she says before leaving. "You'll be safe in here."

As soon as the door shuts behind her, I go

straight for the desk, searching for the gleam of a bright, red ruby. Instead the glint of a silver picture frame catches my eye. Inside there's a black-and-white photo like the one I saw in Pablo's scrapbook, of Tía Abuela and Josefina when they were young.

Engraved along the bottom edge of the frame are the words "Amigas para siempre."

"Friends forever," I say to myself.

This doesn't seem like the kind of thing Josefina would keep on her desk if she were jealous. In fact, it makes me think she might really *like* Tía Abuela.

And she must really *love* being a librarian, I realize. Taped above Josefina's desk are dozens of handwritten notes. *Thank you for the library tour! Thank you for helping me find the perfect book! Thank you for reading to our class!* There are drawings too, some in crayon, some in marker. Even in the drawings that are really scribbly, I can still make out Josefina's long gray hair and her cat-shaped pendant.

Pablo Blanco was wrong. Josefina didn't want to steal the spotlight. It shines on her right here in the library.

I am about to sneak back out to tell him this, when I hear Josefina's footsteps. I jump away from her desk as she's opening the door.

"It's lucky I always keep one of these in my car in case I come across a stray on my drive home." She's holding a pet carrier! "Let's get you inside so you'll be all ready to go when our friends from the animal rescue get here."

I can't let Josefina trap me in the carrier. For one thing, I won't fit! For another, I'll be caught! I bolt.

"Stop!" Josefina yells. "I wish I could let you stay here, but I can't."

I race through the STAFF ONLY doors—which, fortunately, Josefina propped open—to the circulation desk and jump behind it. I try to yank off the sweatshirt hood, but it snags on my barrette.

It isn't long before Josefina catches up. "There you are!" She waves a piece of cheese at me. "Here, Kitty-Cat," she says. "It's Swiss, from my lunch. I'll share it with you if you'll just climb into this cozy carrier."

I have to get out of the sweatshirt. But not where Josefina—or anyone else—can see.

I scurry around the desk, then jump over the study table.

I zigzag around the computer stations.

I dart past the boy looking for summer reading books, knocking over the stack he has piled up.

I scramble through the center of the story time circle. Babies wiggle out of their parents' laps and crawl after me. Carlos leads the pack. "Kitty!" he yells.

Things couldn't possibly get any worse. Babies are chasing me from one direction, Josefina from the other.

I back up until I bump against the dress stand. I am cornered.

I have no choice. I'm about to unzip the sweatshirt—about to reveal the secret of the magic sewing kit.

But then Josefina the Librarian shrieks.

"A spider!"

She kicks at something black and crawly. The thing shoots up into the air, then lands on my head. I pluck it off. Josefina was wrong. It isn't a spider, but I'm just as surprised by it as she is.

Josefina backs away, giving me one last chance to make an escape.

Coco's skateboard is still standing just inside the library entrance. If I can get to it, I might be able to roll away fast enough that Josefina can't catch me—if I don't fall off, that is.

I take a deep breath and race for the skateboard. I pull it away from the wall and jump on. Then, just as the animal rescue volunteer opens the library's front door, I push off with my foot and sail right past him.

I count in my head.

One! Two! Three!

I'm doing it! I'm skateboarding!

Four! Five! Six!

Not until I get to seven do I notice the planter box coming closer and closer.

Too close.

I crash and tumble into an azalea bush.

· CHAPTER 12 ·

ℒost

I walk back into the library, out of breath. My sweatshirt is crumpled under my arm.

Pablo rushes toward me. "Where have you been? You will never believe what you just missed—it was like a scene straight out of *Curse of the Panther*."

He stops and frowns. "What happened to your hair?"

I touch my head. Curls spring out from my temples. I pull an azalea blossom out from behind my ear.

"And your shirt?" he asks. "You're really a mess, you know."

I look down. My shirt is rumpled and half-untucked. I'm not even close to perfectly put together. For once, though, I don't mind.

Pablo smooths his hand over his crisp, white guayabera as if checking to make sure *his* clothes are still in order. He lowers his voice, "So, did you find the ruby in Josefina's office?"

I pat my pocket. "No," I say. "She doesn't have it. But I think I know who does." Not Josefina. Not Pablo.

"Wait, but—" Pablo scratches his head.

"I'll explain everything later," I whisper as Mami walks toward us, pulling the wagon with Baby Carlos asleep inside.

"All that excitement seems to have tired your brother out," Mami says. "Ready to go home, Kitty-Cat?"

"I'm ready."

Outside we wave goodbye to Josefina and the animal rescue volunteer, who are poking around the azalea bushes, looking for a lost cat they'll never find. At least I hope they won't.

Just to be safe, I clutch the sweatshirt even tighter.

"Did you get a look at that cat?" Mami asks as we trudge up the hill. "I'm almost certain it was the same one that was hanging around our front porch the other day."

"Hmm," I reply. Not quite a yes, and not exactly a no.

· CHAPTER 13 ·

The Start

Tía Abuela sits in the rocking chair, sewing. Light from the reading lamp winks off her needle.

"What are you working on?" I ask.

She holds up a white blouse with a square sailor collar.

"Tía Abuela! That's not a magic shirt, is it? Un disfraz?"

She raises an eyebrow above her dark glasses.

I lower my voice. "You're not going to trick people

into believing you're a real sailor, are you?"

Tía Abuela throws back her head and laughs. Her sunglasses nearly slip off, but she catches them with her fingertips. "Por favor! Of course not, Kitty-Cat."

I kneel on the carpet in front of her. With my fingertip I trace the neat line of stitches she has already sewn on the shirt.

"Missing something," I say finally.

Tía Abuela tilts her head. "The shirt? I know it's a little plain, Kitty-Cat, but I can't exactly wear an evening gown at sea."

I shake my head. "No, *you're* missing something."

I reach into my pocket and pull out a fake eyelash. The one Josefina mistook for a spider. I drop it onto the nightstand.

Tía Abuela lifts her sunglasses to the top of her head. Just as I suspected, one of her eyelids is bare.

"Ah," Tía Abuela says. "I wondered where that went."

"It was in the library," I explain. "Underneath the Dragon Dress. That's how I knew *you* were the one who took the ruby. But I still don't know *why*."

Tía Abuela sighs. "I've never sailed before, and I was beginning to get nervous," she confesses. "I wanted something to remind me that, at one time, I had never sewn before. But I learned how, stitch by stitch. And the only way to finish a masterpiece like the Dragon Dress . . ."

I complete the sentence for her. ". . . is to start."

"Así es," Tía Abuela agrees. *That's right.* Slowly

she lifts an edge of the sailor collar. The ruby sparkles underneath.

She explains how, knowing Josefina would keep her secret, she went to the library early to take a jewel from the Dragon Dress. That must have been when she lost the eyelash. "I didn't think anyone would notice," she says. "I should have known *you* would."

Downstairs the front door opens. Seconds later Tía Abuela and I hear the *rrrrrrrooooolllSMACK* of Coco's skateboard on the sidewalk.

My head snaps up.

"Ándale," Tía Abuela says, picking up her sewing again.

I hesitate. I want to go. Only, I know it will be a long time before I can take another sewing lesson from Tía Abuela.

"But you're leaving tomorrow," I say. "And I still need practice."

"A *lot* of practice." Tía Abuela nods.

Then she winks. "Mi amiga Josefina can help. She's starting a new Stitch and Share group at the library. She'll be expecting you at the first meeting. Don't be late."

As if I am *ever* late.

I stop at my bedroom before heading outside. I already have my sweatshirt, but there's something else I need: Coco's flannel.

Not for un disfraz. I'll become a skater for real. With practice. Even if it means I have to mess up a lot more.

Instead I toss the shirt back into my sister's closet. Right where it belongs. Then I grab my helmet and race outside to try again.

Acknowledgments

It was my grandmother Mary Espinoza who taught me to sew. Without her patient and steady hands, this story would not be possible. I am forever grateful to her and to my Nana Josephine, to whom this book is dedicated, for showing me the many forms, some quieter than others, that creativity can take.

Mil gracias to my agent, Jennifer Laughran, who saw what this book could be, and to Alyson Heller, whose love for the family story at the heart

• *Acknowledgments* •

of *Catalina Incognito* shone through in her wise and brilliant editing. I feel incredibly lucky to have worked with illustrator Gladys José, who brought Catalina to life with such charm and, yes, attention to detail! And with designer Laura DiSiena, Elizabeth Mims, Olivia Ritchie, Amelia Jenkins, Valerie Garfield, Kristin Gilson, and everyone else on the Aladdin team.

Finally, thank you to David, Alice, and Soledad. You inspire me all the time.

Turn the page for a sneak peek at Catalina's next magical adventure!

First Day

I have already slurped the last sugary drops of cereal milk off my spoon by the time my big sister, Coco, stumbles to the table.

She yawns and rubs her eyes, then asks, "You're already dressed, Cat?"

"Of course I am." It's the first day of school, after all. Last night I spent two hours organizing my backpack, filling the pouches and pockets with freshly sharpened pencils, never-used erasers, and notebooks with nothing but blank pages inside. Everything is perfectly put together.

Stuffing a backpack with new school supplies is one of my all-time favorite activities. Which means the day before school starts is one of my all-time favorite days of the year.

"But it's so early," Coco whines.

"It's never too early to be prepared," I answer.

Papi sets a bowl of cereal in front of Coco while I carry my empty bowl to the sink.

"Buenos días!" he greets her.

"Ugh," Coco moans.

Baby Carlos, our little brother, bangs his palms against his high chair tray, and Papi drops a few chunks of strawberry onto it. Carlos picks one up and mashes it in his fist.

Even though his sticky hands can't reach me, I still take a big step backward. Just in case.

Mami walks into the kitchen dressed in purple scrubs, all set for her shift at the nursing home.

"Are you excited to start middle school?" she asks, ruffling Coco's sleep-tangled hair.

Coco shrugs.

No one asks if I'm excited to start third grade. Maybe they think it will be just like any other year. Unlike Coco, I'm not going to a new school. But there will still be a new classroom, a new teacher, and—according to my best friend, and biggest rival, Pablo Blanco—a new kid. He heard all about her because his mom is the room parent.

Just one more reason to get to school early. Then *I'll* get to meet the new girl before anyone else does. Even Pablo.

I check to make sure my double-knotted shoelaces haven't come undone, then swing my backpack over my shoulder.

"See you later!" I announce.

Carlos gurgles and waves his gooey hand. Mami and Papi walk over to hug me goodbye.

"Have a wonderful day, mija," Papi says.

"I can't wait to hear all about it," Mami adds, and kisses my forehead.

"Wait!" Coco's mouth is full of frosted wheat squares. "What's the hurry? Give me a few more minutes, and I'll walk with you. Like always."

My hand hovers over the doorknob. Coco and I used to walk to school together every day. But I never thought she actually *wanted* to.

"But we don't go to the same school anymore, remember?" I say, turning the knob.

"We can walk to the corner at least," Coco persists. "I'll even let you ride my skateboard."

Hmm. Coco has been teaching me to ride her skateboard all summer. But only in front of our house. She's never offered to let me ride it anywhere else before.

Even Mami and Papi are surprised.

"Did you hear that, Kitty-Cat?" Papi asks. "Coco says you can ride her skateboard!"

I am tempted to tell Coco yes.

I am tempted to tell Papi to quit calling me "Kitty-Cat."

But, *no*, I decide. There isn't time. I need to get to school. I only have one chance to be the first person to meet the new girl. Then I'll get to introduce her to everyone else. Maybe our teacher will even pick me to show her around school.

"Thanks anyway, Coco," I say. "Maybe tomorrow."

I am stepping out the door when Coco stops me *again*.

"You're wearing *that*?"

My shoulders drop. I hoped no one would notice.

"Didn't you say you were getting too old for all the kitten stuff?" Coco continues.

Slowly I turn around. Coco is pointing at the gray sweatshirt tied around my waist. Two kitten ears and a diamond-shaped patch of white fur are sewn to the hood.

"At least I don't sleep in it too," I say, pointing back at the old flannel shirt Coco *never* takes off.

Coco straightens the collar. "This shirt is *lucky*."

"Well, this sweatshirt," I answer, "is . . . *special*."

"That's right," Mami says. She wraps her arm around my shoulders and squeezes. "Tía Abuela sewed the ears on herself. And I'm sure Kitty-Cat likes wearing it because she misses Tía Abuela. Isn't that right?"

I nod. Tía Abuela is my great-aunt. Her name is Catalina Castañeda just like mine. She used to be a famous telenovela actress. Ever since she retired,

Tía Abuela spends most of her time traveling the world. She doesn't come to our house on the hill in Valle Grande very often, so I *do* miss her.

But that's not the only reason why this sweatshirt is special.

On her last visit Tía Abuela gave me a musty old sewing kit in a red velvet pouch. Inside is a needle and spool of silvery thread. They don't sew regular clothes, though. They create magical disguises. Like this sweatshirt. As soon as I zip it up and pull on the hood, I'll look exactly like an *actual* cat. Over the summer I even used my disfraz to solve a major mystery. So far I haven't shared the secret of the sewing kit with *anyone*.

Before she left on her latest adventure, Tía Abuela warned me that the magic would only be as strong as my stitches. Since I'm still learning, I haven't been able to sew a new disfraz yet. That's why I'm stuck with this one. Even if I *am* getting too old for all this kitten stuff.

I look down at my watch. "Better go," I say. "You know how I feel about being late."

Mami and Papi shudder. Even Coco stops arguing.

I smile to myself and scamper down the front porch steps and out to the sidewalk. Once I'm a few houses down, where I'm sure my family can't see me, I duck behind a mailbox.

I look left and right to make sure no one is watching. I put on the sweatshirt and zip it to my chin. Then I lift the hood over my head. A chill runs up my spine.

I stand and glance down at my shadow on the pavement. It's not the shadow of a girl anymore. It's the shadow of a cat.

I am *incognito*.

Can DOMINGUITA learn to be the hero of her own adventures?

EBOOK EDITIONS AVAILABLE

Aladdin

simonandschuster.com/kids